CARLA CASSIDY

Mercenary's Perfect Mission

ROMANTIC
SUSPENSE

Special thanks and acknowledgment to Carla Cassidy for her contribution to the Perfect, Wyoming miniseries.

Recycling programs
for this product may
not exist in your area.

ISBN-13: 978-0-373-27778-0

MERCENARY'S PERFECT MISSION

www.Harlequin.com

Printed in U.S.A.

Books by Carla Cassidy

Harlequin Romantic Suspense

CARLA CASSIDY

is an award-winning author who has written more than one hundred books for Silhouette Books and Harlequin Books. In 1995 she won Best Silhouette Romance from *RT Book Reviews* for *Anything for Danny*. In 1998 she also won a Career Achievement Award for Best Innovative Series from *RT Book Reviews*.

Carla believes the only thing better than curling up with a good book to read is sitting down at the computer with a good story to write. She's looking forward to writing many more books and bringing hours of pleasure to readers.

Chapter 1

The Wyoming woods atop the tall mountains that cradled the town of Cold Plains were just beginning to take on a fall cast of color. This worked perfectly with the camouflage long-sleeved T-shirt and pants that Micah Grayson wore as he made his way through the thick brush and trees.

Although a gun holster rode his shoulder, he held his gun tight in his hand. Despite the fact that he had only been hiding out in the mountainous woods for two days and nights, he'd quickly learned that danger could come in the blink of an eye, a danger that might require the quick tic of his index finger on the trigger.

Twilight had long ago fallen but a near-full moon overhead worked as an additional enemy when it came to using the shield of darkness for cover.

As an ex-mercenary, Micah knew how to learn the terrain and use the weather to his advantage. He knew how to keep the reflection of the moonlight off his skin so as not to alert anyone to his presence. He could move through a bed of dry leaves and not make a sound. He could be wearing a black suit in a snowstorm and still figure out a way to become invisible.

The first twenty-four hours that he'd been in the woods he'd learned natural landmarks, studied pitfalls and figured out places he thought would make good hidey-holes if needed. He'd also come face-to-face with a moose, heard the distant call of a wolf and seen several elk and deer.

He now moved with the stealth of a big cat toward the rocky cliff he'd discovered the night before. As he crept low and light on his feet, he kept alert, his ears open for any alien sound that might not belong to the forest.

Despite the relative coolness of the night, a trickle of sweat trekked down the center of his back. During his thirty-eight years of life, Micah had faced a thousand life-threatening situations, the latest of which had been a bullet to his head that had sent him into a coma for months.

When he finally reached the rocky bluff he looked down at the lights dotting the little valley, the lights of the small town of Cold Plains, Wyoming. His brother Samuel's town. Micah reached up and touched the scar, now barely discernible through his thick dark hair on the left side of his head, the place where Samuel's henchman, Dax Roberts, had shot him while Micah had sat in his car. Dax had left him for dead.

Fortunately for Micah he hadn't died, but had come out of a three-month coma with the fierce, driving need for revenge against the fraternal twin he'd always somehow known was a dangerous, narcissistic sociopath.

Unfortunately, Samuel was also charming and slick and powerful, making him a natural leader that people wanted to follow.

Five months ago Micah had been sitting in a small-town Kansas coffee shop where he'd landed after his last mission for a little downtime when he'd seen a face almost identical to his own flash across the television mounted to the wall.

Stunned, he'd watched a news story unfold that told him his brother Samuel was being questioned by the FBI and local police in connection with the murders of five women found all across Wyoming. All the women had one thing in common: Cold Plains, the town where his wealthy, motivational-speaker brother wielded unbelievable influence and power.

Micah had immediately contacted the FBI and been put in touch with an agent named Hawk Bledsoe. The two had made arrangements to meet the next day but, before Micah could make that meeting, he'd caught the bullet to his head.

He'd been in the coma for ninety-three long days and it had taken him another two months to feel up to the task he knew he had to do—take out Samuel before he could destroy any more people and lives.

Which was why he'd spent these last two days and nights in the woods adjacent to Cold Plains.

Minutes before he'd made his way to the bluff, he'd met with his FBI contact, Hawk. Hawk had grown up in Cold Plains and after years of being away from his hometown had returned to discover that the rough-around-the-edges place where he'd grown up as son of the town drunk had transformed into something eerily perfect. A town run by a group of people who others referred to under their breaths as the Devotees and their leader, the movie-star handsome, but frightening and dangerous Samuel Grayson.

For the past two nights Micah and Hawk had met at dusk in the woods so Hawk could keep Micah apprised of what was going on in town and how the FBI investigation into Samuel's misdeeds was progressing.

As he thought about everything Hawk had shared with him over the last two days, a dull throb began at the scar in the side of his head. He drew in several deep, long breaths, attempting to will away one of the killer migraines that the bullet had left behind.

He turned and started off the bluff, deciding to make his way down the mountain, closer to town. The only time he dared to do a little reconnaissance of the layout of the town was at night. He knew that if anyone caught sight of him it would be reported back to Samuel, and the last thing Micah wanted Samuel to know was that he was not only still alive but he was also here and working with the FBI to bring him down.

As always, he moved silently, knowing that the woods held many secrets. Just the night before, he'd stumbled upon two women amid the brush and trees. Darcy Craven had fainted at the sight of him, assuming he was his brother, but the woman with her, June Farrow, had recognized that he wasn't Samuel and had taken him to the safe house located in an area called Hidden Valley.

The safe house and surrounding land, only accessible by hiking or helicopter, had become an important haven for those trying to escape Samuel and his minions. The woods weren't just filled with those trying to escape the small town, but also dangerous hunters tracking them down.

Samuel had to be stopped. The words had reverberated in his head the moment he'd awakened from his coma and that thought was the driving force that got him up each morning, his final thought before falling asleep at night.

He froze as he thought he heard a sound someplace to his left. It sounded like a baby's cry; there for just a moment and then gone as if stolen from the gentle night breeze. He remained still, his index finger ready to fire the gun gripped tight in his hand if necessary.

Micah wasn't given to flights of fantasy. He knew he'd heard something. It was possible that it had been some sort of animal, but there was no way he intended to leave this area until he found the source of the sound.

There were hunters in the woods, but Micah was one, too, and if he managed to get to one of the men who worked for Samuel, he'd turn them over to the FBI to help them build a case against the man, hopefully a case that would avenge the deaths of the five women Micah knew in his heart his brother was responsible for killing.

The noise came again…a quick cry that was just as quickly gone. The darkness of the night seemed to press in around him as he targeted in on the area where he thought the sound had originated.

The moon slivered through the tree branches here and there, filtering down enough illumination to be both a little bit helpful and definitely dangerous. Micah kept to the dark shadows as he made his way toward the noise.

Somebody was in the woods, of that he was certain. He wouldn't put it past Samuel to arrange for one of his minions to make the noises he'd heard, hoping to draw somebody out of the safe house, hoping that somebody could be taken into custody and then be forced to give up the location of the place of safety.

His heart took on the slow, steady beat of a trained soldier as he advanced forward. He'd just stepped around a tree when he saw her. Despite the fact that she was backed into the brush, her white-blond hair served as a beacon calling to the moonlight.

In an instant, he took in everything. Small and petite, her jeans and blouse appeared dirty and her hair was tangled with bits of leaves and brush caught in the curly length. She held a baby in a sling across her chest and a sharp, pointed stick raised in her hand.

If she thought that puny stick might be used as a weapon against him, she was sadly mistaken. Micah could have that stick out of her hand and broken in half before she ever saw him coming.

As he stepped close enough for her to see him, she looked up and gasped, her green eyes widening in abject terror.

"I won't tell," she exclaimed fervently. "Please don't hurt me. I swear I won't tell anyone what I saw. Just let me have my other son and we'll go far away from here. I'll never speak your name again." Her voice cracked as she focused on his gun and he realized she believed he was Samuel.

Certainly it was dark enough that anyone could mistake him for his brother. When the brothers were together it was easy to see the subtle differences between them. Micah's face was slightly thinner, his features more chiseled than those of his brother.

At the moment, Micah knew Samuel kept his hair cut neat and tidy while Micah's long hair was tied back. He reached up and pulled the rawhide strip, allowing his hair to fall from its binds.

The woman gasped once again. "You aren't him... but you look like him. Who are you?" Her voice still held fear as she dropped the stick and protectively clutched the baby closer to her chest.

"Who are *you?*" he countered. He wasn't about to be taken in by a pale-haired angel with big green eyes in this evil place where angels probably couldn't exist.

"I'm Olivia Conner, and this is my son Sam." Tears filled her eyes. "I have another son, but he's still in town. I couldn't get to him before I ran away. I've heard rumors that there was a safe house somewhere, but I've been in the woods for two days and I can't find it." The tears spilled a little faster. "I need to get someplace safe, where Sam can get something to eat and I can go back into town and get my other son."

Micah was unmoved by her tears and by her story. He knew how devious his brother could be and Micah would do everything possible to protect the location of the safe house. There was only one way to know for sure if she was one of Samuel's "Devotees."

"I need to see your right hip," he said.

Once again her eyes opened wide, but it was obvious she knew why he'd made the demand. The people closest to Samuel, the people who were a part of his "cult" were all tattooed on their right hip with a letter *D.* Before he took her anywhere, he needed to see that she wasn't wearing Samuel's mark.

She pulled the sling over her neck and placed the baby on the ground where he sat up and gazed at Micah with a drooling grin. Olivia stood, dwarfed by Micah's six feet two and as she looked up at him, he saw the fear that still simmered in the depths of her eyes.

Her slender fingers trembled as they unfastened her jeans and slipped them down low enough to expose one pale hip. Micah pulled a flashlight from his pocket and shone it on the area, wanting to be absolutely sure that he didn't miss any tattoo that would mark her as one of Samuel's closest followers.

Confident that there was nothing there, he motioned her to refasten her jeans. "You never told me who you are," she said as she fastened the jeans and then pulled on the sling and the child back against her chest.

"And you never told me exactly how you came to be in the middle of the woods in the dead of the night with only one of your two children," he countered.

In the light of the moon he saw her eyes darken and fear once again shine from the depths. She hesitated, as if unsure what to tell him, then finally released a weary sigh. "I was on my way to the child care center to pick up my three-year-old son Ethan when I saw something that shocked me…something that frightened me so badly I just ran. Please, I need help. We're hungry. My baby is hungry."

Micah knew he was a good judge of character and more than once that quality had saved his life. There was a genuine desperation in her eyes, and that, coupled with the absence of the telltale tattoo, allowed him to put away any misgivings about her credibility.

"What was it that you saw that scared you so bad you ran?" he asked.

She lifted her chin a notch and although her lips trembled slightly there was defiance in her stance as she straightened her shoulders and squared off to him. "I'm not saying anything more until I know who you are and what you intend to do with me."

"I'm Micah Grayson, Samuel's brother. I'm here to take him down, but right now I'm going to take you to the safe house. Stay close, move fast and keep quiet." With these words he turned his back to her and began to move.

Samuel's brother.

Those words were enough to shoot complete terror through Olivia's heart. She had no idea if she could trust him or not, but she knew with certainty that she and her baby boy couldn't survive much more time in the woods all alone without food or water. She hadn't slept for two days and nights, afraid of each and every sound the forest made as she'd tried to find the safe house and stay hidden from danger at the same time.

At the moment she felt as if she had no other choice but to trust him and so she hurried after him, her heart pounding a million miles a minute.

The only thing that gave her comfort was that he was leading her in a direction deeper into the woods rather than back toward the little town she'd recently escaped.

She cuddled Sam to her chest, hoping he'd fall asleep. He'd been fussy off and on throughout the evening and she knew he was hungry and tired of the sling. She'd managed to stave off some of his hunger pangs over the last couple days with the snacks she always kept stored in her backpack, but earlier that evening she'd given him the last of the crackers and the last sip of juice.

Nights on the mountain weren't kind at this time of year. Although a September day could be warm and pleasant, the nights turned cold and she hadn't been prepared or equipped with the supplies or the survival skills she'd needed.

She had to trust Micah because she had no other choice. He was a daunting man, tall and with shoulders the size of a small county. In the moonlight his green eyes had looked icy cold—deadly—but she had run out of options.

He kept up a fast pace, moving through the woods like a shadow as she hurried to keep up with him. As he led her to a narrow crevice in the side of the mountain, she realized that if this really was the way to the safe house she would have never been able to find it on her own.

It felt like they had walked for miles in the narrow crevice where only the faint beam of his flashlight lit the way. He paused as they appeared to be at a dead end and once again her heart banged frantically. Had he brought her here to kill her? Was he really working for his brother or had he told the truth and was working against him?

Despite the appearance of a dead end, he twisted his body into a seemingly invisible space and as she followed, she realized they'd entered a cave tunnel. She could feel a faint breeze on her face and knew the end wasn't far.

He paused once again, this time to pull a radio from his pocket. "It's Micah. I'm coming in with two."

"Copy," a faint voice replied.

Micah dropped the radio back in his pocket and moved forward. Within moments they had left the cave and entered a small valley. The moonlight was brighter now and she could see a man standing in front of a rocky entrance of a half-hidden cave.

He was armed, but greeted Micah by name. "I told June you're coming in," he said.

"Thanks, Jesse." Micah grabbed her by the elbow, his big hand warm on her skin.

They went through another small narrow passage and that opened into a huge cave that had been transformed into living quarters.

Olivia felt her mouth drop open as she took in her surroundings. It was like entering an alien world with huge ceilings and furnished comfortably with wood, bone, animal skins and whatever else the forest could yield.

"Follow me," Micah said. "June will probably be in the kitchen area and we have questions for you."

She had plenty of questions for him, too. She'd expected the rumored safe house to be a little cabin in the woods where people were spirited in and out of the area in the middle of the night.

But, as she heard the sound of laughter coming from someplace in the distance and followed Micah through the huge main room where the scent of something cooking wafted in the air, this place felt more like a thriving community than a pit stop on the way to safety.

Micah led her into a kitchen where the focal point of the room was a huge rough-hewn wooden table above which hung a chandelier fashioned from antlers.

A woman stood at a stove stirring what smelled like some sort of stew. She turned at the sight of them and offered Olivia a tentative smile. "Got the news there were two incoming, didn't realize it was really one and a half."

Olivia looked down at Sam, who had fallen asleep against her chest and fought the tears that pressed hot against her eyes.

"She says she's been in the woods for two days," Micah said as he gestured Olivia into a chair at the table.

"And you must be starving," the tall, willowy, red-haired woman said as Olivia took off her backpack and sank into one of the chairs. Micah took the chair next to her and she was instantly aware of two things—he smelled like the forest, fresh, wild, yet clean and utterly male. And even though he looked amazingly like his brother, Samuel Grayson was really just a pale imitation of the handsome, hard-featured man seated to her right.

"I'm June Farrow," the woman said as she set a bowl of hot stew in front of Olivia. "And I'd be more than happy to hold that sleeping little boy so you can eat."

Olivia looked down at Sam and for a moment the last thing she wanted to do was relinquish possession of the one child she had with her. Once again as she thought of her missing three-year-old, her eyes welled up with tears that she desperately tried to control.

"What's his name?" June asked softly.

"Sam. His name is Sam." Olivia pulled the child from the front sling and handed him into June's awaiting arms. She had to trust these people, she had no choice and the scent of the food cramped her empty stomach. She'd had nothing to eat for the last two days, afraid that if she took a single bite of anything that had been in her backpack, it might mean Sam going hungry.

Micah sat silently as she ate. She tried not to shovel

the savory stew into her mouth like a wild animal. She had no idea what exactly was in the stew, but nothing had ever tasted so good.

When she was finished she looked at June. "Is there milk? I have a bottle for Sam in my backpack but he emptied it the first night we were in the woods."

The area where she sat was warmer than it had been outside and with her belly full, all she really wanted to do was sleep. She'd only had unanticipated fitful dozes while in the forest; she'd been too afraid to allow herself any real sleep. The forest had been filled with critters, both animal and human.

"How about I get a bottle ready for Sam and put him down in the nursery?" June asked.

Panic once again clawed up Olivia's throat. "Nursery? Where is that? What, exactly, is this place?"

"You're safe here and nobody will hurt you or your son," Micah finally spoke. "Why don't you and June get the boy settled in for the night and then the three of us will talk some more."

Olivia hesitated for a long moment, so many questions whirling around in her head, coupled with the crushing fear for the child she had left behind.

She finally got up from the table and rummaged in the now nearly empty backpack for the empty bottle. June handed Sam back to her and Olivia watched as the woman washed the bottle and then filled it with milk. "Come with me," she then said.

The cave was a maze of rooms, some small, some much larger, some with wooden doors and some without. The temperature was slightly cooler away from the kitchen area, but not unpleasantly so.

They finally came to a medium-sized room that held

several cribs and child-sized cots. "We have a couple three-year-olds, but they're sleeping with their mommy in another room, so right now he's the only little one we have here," June said as she motioned for Olivia to place Sam in one of the cribs.

Sam awakened and as always gave his mother a beatific smile and then when he saw the bottle June held, his fingers worked in a gimme fashion. "Bot," he exclaimed.

June smiled and gave him the bottle and as he began to drink it, his eyes drifted closed once again. The two women backed out of the nursery and June showed her the room next door. "We'll put you in here, that way you can hear if he needs anything throughout the night."

This area was small, with a door and a double bed covered with what appeared to be clean sheets and a lightweight blanket. A small rustic wooden table sat next to the bed with an oil lantern burning to light the room. "I'm afraid it isn't exactly the Ritz, but we all manage."

"It's fine," Olivia replied, still feeling as if she'd entered a surreal world she didn't quite understand.

"We'd better get back to Micah. He's probably chewing off his own arm waiting to ask you some questions."

When they headed to the kitchen, the scent of freshly brewed coffee filled the air. Micah was seated where he'd been when they had left, but three cups of coffee were on the table. "I wasn't sure how you drank yours," he said to Olivia.

"Black is fine." She curled her fingers around the warmth of the mug and then looked at June. "What is this place and what are all of you doing here?"

"The cave was built a long time ago by an architect

who went crazy and became an eccentric survivalist—decided to prepare for the end of the world. He was something of a genius when it came to using the natural resources accessible in the mountains. Rumor has it that he died when he'd finished construction and it was left to a distant relative of his. About five years ago, when we realized what was happening in Cold Plains, we knew we'd need a place of safety so we contacted the owner who told us to do whatever we wanted with it. We did a little refurbishing to make it once again livable and here we are," June explained.

Olivia was aware of Micah's dark gaze lingering on her, but she wasn't finished getting answers from June. "So, this is about an investigation of some sort? Are you a police officer of some kind?"

June smiled. "Heavens no. I'm just a widow who, years ago, lost my family to a cult and now I've made it my life's mission running safe houses for members who leave and need a place to hide and to be deprogrammed."

"A cult? But Cold Plains is just a beautiful small town, a wonderful place to raise children. It's a place of health and prosperity." She frowned, recognizing she was parroting Samuel's words.

She tried not to think about the fact that she'd planned on getting the *D* tattoo on her hip before she left Cold Plains and that she'd been completely devoted to Samuel Grayson—until that moment two nights ago when everything she'd believed about the man had exploded apart.

"It's definitely a cult and it's run by a very dangerous man," Micah said.

"Your brother."

He nodded and his green eyes transformed to a darker shade like the deepest forest shadows.

"You look a lot like him," she replied.

"An unfortunate accident of genes. We're fraternal twins. I'm here working with the FBI to bring down Samuel and all his cult enforcers."

Olivia stared first at June and then back at Micah, trying to wrap her mind around the fact that the perfect little town she'd called home was actually run by a group of evil "cult" members. "It's a beautiful town. Everything shines with prosperity and newness. They're even drawing in celebrities and big investors. I lived in a charming little house and had a great job. My children were happy and had the best health care available." Once again she was aware that she was saying what she'd been told, what had been almost a mantra of the townspeople who followed Samuel's teachings.

Still, she didn't need to be deprogrammed by anyone. Her break with anything to do with Samuel and his messages and his way of life had happened in a single heart-stopping instant.

"So, what are you doing here? Why were you hiding out in the woods looking for the safe house?" Micah asked.

Olivia's heart began to beat an unsteady rhythm as she remembered what had happened, what she'd seen two nights before. "I worked at the Community Center as a secretary. That day Sam had been fussy so I'd kept him with me at work. Samuel never minded if I needed to have him with me. As usual Ethan, my three-year-old, had gone to the Cold Plains Day Care."

She took a sip of her coffee, hoping the warmth would heat the icy chill that had suddenly gripped her heart. "I worked a little later than usual, so it was dark when I finally left the Community Center. The day care wasn't far away and I took off walking, knowing that Ethan would be eager to see me and his little brother after such a long day."

Emotion once again pressed tight in her chest, rising up the back of her throat, but she swallowed hard, needing to get through this before she allowed herself to completely fall apart.

She took another sip of the strong coffee as Micah and June waited patiently for her to continue. She set the cup back on the table, aware that her fingers were trembling.

"There was an alley adjacent to the street," she continued. "I saw Samuel and another man standing there talking and I didn't really think too much about it. They didn't look angry or upset, but as the man turned to leave, Samuel pulled a gun and shot him in the back of his head. There was no sound. He must have used a silencer, but as the man fell to the ground, I ran."

She had run like the wind, with panic stealing away all rational thought. Get away. Get away, that had been her only thought. She'd dashed away, praying that Samuel hadn't seen her, fearing not just for her own life but for Sam's life, too.

"Did Samuel see you?" Micah asked as he leaned forward.

A trembling began in the very center of her very soul. "I don't know. I didn't stick around to find out. I just ran, with no thought, with no particular plan in mind. I'd heard rumors that there was a safe house someplace up the mountain but I had no idea how difficult it might be to find. I went for Ethan, but the day care was dark, empty, and I didn't have time to locate him. I was afraid that if Samuel had seen me, I'd never make it to my son. And I'd be putting Sam in danger, as well."

"You need to give this information to Hawk," Micah said. "An eyewitness account to murder is just what we need to get Samuel into custody."

"Who is Hawk?" Olivia asked.

"Hawk Bledsoe. He's a native from Cold Plains but he's now an FBI agent working on the case."

"And what exactly is the case?" Confusion coupled with exhaustion made everything difficult to comprehend for her at the moment.

"The main investigation is into the killing of five women. We believe Samuel is responsible for their murders."

Olivia gasped and shot a hand to her head as an ache began to pound at her temples. She'd heard some vague rumors, but she hadn't believed any of them. Still, as terrible as it sounded, at the moment she didn't want to hear about murdered women. She didn't want to hear about cults and Samuel.

She dropped her hand back to the table and looked Micah in his cold, dark green eyes. She raised her chin, refusing to be intimidated by him and firm in the decision she'd just made. "I'm not talking to anyone until I get my son back."

And then to her horror she burst into tears.

Chapter 2

"Can we trust her?" Hawk asked Micah an hour after Micah had radioed for Hawk to see him. The two stood in their meeting place, a small rocky area next to the stream that eventually made its way into Cold Plains where it became Fog Creek. There was a tree nearby that had been scarred by a lightning strike at some point in the distant past.

Fog Creek was important to Samuel. His cohorts bottled the creek water and sold it to everyone who attended Samuel's many seminars. It was rumored to have magical healing properties, but Micah knew the only thing it really did was line his brother's pockets.

"She seems like the real deal," Micah said as he thought of the pretty blonde. Once June had led her away from the kitchen to show her the shower facility and to find some clean clothes for her to wear, he'd taken off to meet Hawk and let him know this latest development.

Hawk's brown eyes narrowed as he quickly raked a hand through his sandy-colored hair. "It would be just like him, you know—to use a woman and a child to try to find the whereabouts of the safe house."

"Believe me, that thought crossed my mind," Micah replied drily. "But her story had a ring of truth and she seemed genuinely traumatized." He quickly told Micah what Olivia had told them about seeing Samuel shoot the man in the alley. "She freaked and she ran and, in her terror, she had to leave behind one of her kids who was no longer at day care."

"A shot to the back of the man's head." Hawk leaned against the tree behind him. "Sound familiar?"

"Too damned familiar," Micah replied darkly. They both knew that Samuel's favorite form of murder was a bullet to the back of the head; clean, cold and efficient. Unfortunately, knowing it and proving it were two different things. And so far, Samuel had managed to evade all efforts to tie him personally to anything nefarious that was happening in the town.

"Is it possible Samuel kept one of her kids as leverage and then sent her out here to spy on us?" Hawk asked.

"You know with Samuel anything is possible," Micah replied, his stomach churning at the possibility.

"I'll check her out and if she is the real deal, then a statement from her would go a long way in helping us build our case against Samuel," Hawk said.

"She already told me she isn't talking to anyone official until she gets her other son back."

"Are you sure there really is another son?" Hawk's distrust was warranted. If there was one thing Micah had quickly learned in his brief time working with the

FBI, it was that nobody in the town of Cold Plains could be trusted.

"The only thing I'm sure of at the moment is that she won't be left alone until we're sure we can trust her. June or one of the others won't let her out of their sight," Micah replied.

"I'll do a little snooping around in town and see if I can definitely confirm her identity and her story," Hawk replied as he shoved himself off the tree where he'd been leaning. "It shouldn't be too hard to find out if the secretary for the Community Center has suddenly disappeared and left one of her kids behind, although it might be more difficult to identify who Samuel shot."

"And it's a sure bet that if Samuel didn't know she saw what he did, he'll definitely wonder what drove her away from town without Ethan and he'll be frantic to find her." Micah felt the muscles in his jaw tighten as he thought of his brother, who had grown more and more dangerous with each passing day, especially since feeling the pressure of the investigation.

If Olivia Conner was truly who and what she said she was, then if Samuel found her, she would probably wind up like the other five dead women…with a bullet in the back of her head.

Five murdered women and any number of other deaths, all attributed to Samuel and his cult henchmen. Devotees, that's what Samuel called the people who followed him and his teachings like blind sheep. Some of them were simply deluded, others desperate to belong to something bigger than themselves, but there were a handful of Samuel's closest followers who were simply evil at their very hearts and souls.

"I'll check in with you in the morning, let you know

what I've found out," Hawk said and a moment later he'd disappeared into the darkness.

Micah remained where he stood, the memory of one particular woman filling his head. He rarely allowed himself to go back in time to when he'd been in high school and ridiculously in love with Johanna Tate.

Even now after all these years he could still remember the vanilla scent of her straight black hair and the long lashes that fringed her pale brown eyes. He still remembered the sound of her laughter, a melodious sound that had melted his heart the first time he'd heard it.

He'd loved her with all the lust and passion that a teenage boy could own. At the time he'd thought her the woman he'd marry and build a family with, the one who would be at his side throughout his life.

Unfortunately, she'd only been his for a brief period of time before Samuel had seduced her away from him. Even after all these years Micah still felt the pain, the rage, of what his brother had done.

He'd seduced her, brought her to Cold Plains where she had been rumored to be Samuel's main girlfriend, and then she'd been killed with a bullet to the back of her head, her body found eighty miles away in Eden, Wyoming.

Despite the distance between Samuel and where her body had been found, Micah knew in his gut that his brother was responsible for her death.

He now headed back to the safe house, a burning in the pit of his stomach as he tried not to think about how many other lives his brother had destroyed.

As he drew closer to the house, his thoughts turned to another woman, one with eyes the color of the forest and hair like spun silk, a woman who had been prepared to attack him with a sharp stick as she'd huddled in the brush with her son.

Olivia Conner. Even with the dirt on her face and leaves in her hair, holding a baby in one arm and a makeshift weapon in the other, Micah had, on some base level, registered the fact that she was an extremely attractive woman. He was vaguely surprised that he'd even noticed. It had been a very long time since a woman had appeared on his radar in any fashion.

At the moment she was potentially an eyewitness to a murder that Samuel had committed. If he could convince her to talk to one of the FBI agents working the case, then her statement might prove invaluable in breaking everything wide open.

Samuel had always been so careful. It was rare for him to get his own hands dirty but, in Olivia Conner, he'd apparently unknowingly allowed an eyewitness to get away. Micah knew the more Samuel recognized a loss of control, the more dangerous he became.

The best thing for everyone was for Olivia to speak to the authorities and give them a statement, and then be spirited away from here and into some sort of pro-tective custody far away from Cold Plains.

It was this thought that filled his head as he slipped back into the cave where June and two other women were seated at the rough-hewn table. Olivia wasn't one of them.

"She took a shower and then went to bed," June said before he could ask. "The poor thing was absolutely exhausted after being in the woods for two nights all alone with her baby."

Micah poured himself a cup of coffee and then joined them at the table. "Hawk is planning on checking out her story. We want to make sure she really is who she says she is."

"Her little boy is a doll. I peeked in on him when I heard they'd arrived," Darcy Craven said.

As always when Micah looked at Darcy with her beautiful long, dark hair and blue eyes, he felt a strange sense of familiarity. Her eyes were those of a woman he'd known a long time ago in his hometown, but then again he couldn't imagine what this young woman would have to do with anyone from his past.

He knew little about Darcy, only that she'd come to Cold Plains seeking news of a mother she'd never known and had developed a romance with Rafe Black, a new doctor in town.

Rafe had shown up in town because the fourth murder victim, Abby Michaels, an old girlfriend of his, had contacted him to tell him he was the father of her three-month-old baby boy. Abby's body had been found in a wooded area in Laramie, fifty miles away from Cold Plains Day Care Center, where she'd worked as a teacher's aide. The baby, now an almost nine-month-old named Devin, had been missing since her disappearance.

A month earlier a little boy had been found by police officer Ford McCall with a note stating that he was Devin Black and needed to be reunited with his father. According to what Micah had heard, Rafe believed he'd finally had a happy ending, not only with his son found but also with a romantic relationship with Darcy.

But, the happy ending had been short-lived. The baby boy had been kidnapped by a man claiming to be the real child's father. A birthmark on the boy had confirmed it. He had said he'd been forced by Samuel and Bo Fargo, the chief of police and Samuel's right-hand man, to give up the boy for the good of the community. He'd done what he'd been told, but couldn't live with his actions.

He'd stolen the baby back from Rafe, leaving the doctor to wonder about the whereabouts of his own son. The man had refused to make any official statements indicting either Samuel or Bo Fargo in the scheme and had disappeared from town soon after.

Even though he and Darcy were still very much in love, Rafe had insisted Darcy go to the safe house until his son could be found again.

There were so many players in this deadly game, and both June and Hawk had spent a lot of time trying to fill Micah in on everything that had been happening both in the town of Cold Plains and in his brother's life.

At night Micah's head spun as he tried to put names with people and figure out who was on their side and who was one of Samuel's Devotees. There were so many people in town that nobody knew exactly where they landed in the grand scheme of things—if they were Samuel's people or not.

In the brief time he'd been in the safe house, Micah had recognized that it was basically a clearinghouse where June helped deprogram those who needed it and the FBI aided in relocating victims to new lives. The people were in transition and most didn't stay too long, but rather were eager to get as far away from Samuel and Cold Plains, Wyoming, as quickly as possible.

He now leaned back in his chair and took a sip of his coffee, his thoughts on the newest members of the house. "If she'll talk to Hawk and some of the other FBI agents, then we could potentially get an arrest warrant for Samuel for the murder she witnessed," he said. "We'd have a reason to get inside his house, maybe find some real concrete evidence to put him away forever."

"I wouldn't push her too hard," June warned. "She seemed pretty fragile."

"This whole situation is fragile," Micah replied drily. "We have five murdered woman that were all tied in one way or another to Cold Plains and Samuel. We have enough additional dead bodies to fill an entire cemetery."

"And missing children and people with disabilities who seem to have vanished into midair," Darcy added, her hauntingly blue eyes darkening.

Micah frowned and took a sip of his coffee. Aside from the murdered women, this was one of the most disturbing things about this case. The streets were filled with only attractive, robust people seemingly not only physically fit but mentally well. There was no sickness, no imperfections of any kind and those who showed signs of either disappeared and were never seen again.

"There are rumors that those people are held in secret rooms or basements, prisoners for the good of the town. The worst part is the children," Darcy said. "I think we've all heard the rumors of children who are born with slight 'defects' or deemed unworthy in some way and are hidden away someplace in town and eventually adopted out."

Her face displayed a myriad of emotions and Micah suspected she was thinking of Rafe Black's missing son. Was he hidden in some secret location in town or had he already been adopted out by Samuel for a huge fee to a couple in another state, another country, desperate for a child?

"Of course, we don't have to worry about anything now that the FBI have arrested some of Samuel's henchmen and they've confessed to the murders of some of the women," June said sarcastically.

Micah snorted. "They might have confessed to being the ones who actually pulled the triggers, but they still refuse to give up Samuel as the brains. Until we can cut off the head of the snake, nobody is safe and we'll never know for sure who in town we can trust." He knew that a man and a woman had been arrested by the FBI and had confessed to some of the murders of the women, but they'd refused to name the man who had given them the orders to commit the crimes.

Once again his thoughts turned to the pretty blonde now sleeping in the depths of the large cave. She was the key. She had the kind of solid information that could put Samuel behind bars.

All he had to do was figure out a way to force her to do the right thing.

Olivia awakened slowly, her brain fuzzy with residual dreams of her childhood. It had not been a particularly good upbringing and the dreams hadn't been pleasant ones.

She'd grown up in a trailer park with her sickly mother who liked to drink. Olivia never knew if her mother was sick because she drank, or drank because she was sick. Her main memories of her youth were of too little food, too little heat and far too much responsibility.

Her mother died when she was twenty-two and Olivia had known two things: she wanted to get as far away from the trailer park as possible and she was desperate to build a different kind of life for herself.

Two children later, abandoned by her boyfriend on Main Street in Cold Plains, Olivia had embraced the town and thought she'd finally come home.

As she thought of that moment in the alley when she'd watched the man she'd believed was her salvation and mentor cold-bloodedly shoot the man in the alley, she had gasped and sat straight up, disoriented for a moment as she looked around.

The cave walls in this room were particularly smooth with a small outcropping of rock that made a natural stone bench against one wall. The small oil-burning lamp still flickered, creating a pool of illumination that allowed her to maneuver easily through the room.

Sam!

Thoughts of her youngest son shot her off the bed. She'd slept in the clothes June had graciously provided her, a pair of jeans, and a T-shirt that was a tad too small across her full breasts.

She knew her hair was probably in wild disarray, but the only thing that mattered at the moment was seeing Sam's smiling face, assuring herself that he was okay.

She couldn't even think about her three-year-old still someplace in Cold Plains. Ethan would probably be scared, needing his mommy and if she dwelled on that thought for too long she'd come completely undone. She had to keep it together, for Sam's sake…for Ethan's sake.

Racing into the room where she'd placed Sam in a crib the night before, she stopped short in the doorway as she saw that the crib was empty. She whirled around, running wildly down a corridor, wondering if perhaps she'd trusted the wrong people after all.

As she wound around corners and ran into blind passageways, her heart banged discordantly, making her half-breathless as she felt like Alice suddenly falling down a rabbit hole.

She whirled around one corner and slammed into a brick wall. The wall was Micah Grayson's hard, muscled chest. "Whoa," he said and grabbed her firmly by the shoulders.

"Where's my son? Where's Sam?" she asked.

He dropped his hands from her shoulders. "I just saw him in the kitchen eating some breakfast."

A shudder of relief swept through her. "Where's the kitchen? This place is like a maze."

He pointed down the nearest passageway. "Go straight and take the left turn. You'll be in the kitchen."

As her panic ebbed, she once again noticed that Micah Grayson wasn't just hard and dangerous looking, but also handsome and sexy in a way that might have affected her under different circumstances.

"Thanks," she said and started to move past him, but he reached out and grabbed her arm before she could scurry away.

"I'd like to speak with you later…after you get some breakfast and settle in." His hand was big…weighty on her forearm.

She frowned. She couldn't imagine what he might want to talk to her about and, if she were perfectly honest with herself, she would admit that something about him unsettled her more than a little bit. All she really wanted to do was make sure Sam was safe and then figure out some sort of plan to return to Cold Plains and retrieve Ethan.

She wasn't interested in whatever investigation they were conducting in the town. She just wanted to have her children safe and with her and then she'd go from there.

"Olivia?"

Her name sounded strange on his lips, reminding her that she knew nothing about this man, these people and the touch of his big hand on her arm felt too warm, oddly intimate.

She pulled away from him and took a step backward. "Obviously I'm not interested anyplace but the kitchen for the time being. You can find me there after breakfast."

This time when she turned to walk away he didn't stop her although she imagined she could feel his piercing green eyes lingering on her back.

She breathed a sigh of relief as she entered the kitchen where June sat at the table with her coffee and Sam was locked into a high chair happily smooshing scrambled eggs into his mouth.

"Mama!" he exclaimed with a happy eggy grin as she entered the room.

"Sammy," she replied and planted a kiss on the top of his forehead. She offered a tentative smile to June. "I had a moment of panic when I woke up and didn't find him in his crib."

"I'm sorry. I didn't mean to frighten you. He woke up earlier and you were still sleeping so soundly, so I figured I'd get him up and change his diaper and see about a little breakfast for him." June smiled sympathetically. "I knew you were exhausted from your time hiding out so I hated to wake you when he got up."

"Thank you for taking care of him," Olivia said as she sank down at the table. She still felt as if she'd entered some strange subterranean world filled with people in crisis. She was in crisis. There was a simmering anxiety inside her that threatened to burst into full-blown panic, but she used every ounce of her ability in an attempt to hold herself together.

"Coffee?" June asked as she rose from the table.

"I can get it," Olivia replied. "You don't have to wait on me."

"Nonsense," June replied and waved Olivia back into the chair. "As an official member of the household, you get one day of acclimating yourself before we assign you any duties. Scrambled eggs?"

"If it's not too much trouble," she replied, feeling guilty, but yet oddly relieved that for the moment somebody else was in charge.

What she wanted more than anything was to eat breakfast, regain her strength and have a chance to formulate some sort of a plan to get Ethan out of Cold Plains. Unfortunately, part of the problem was she wasn't sure where he would be. The last time she'd seen him had been when she'd left him at the Cold Plains Day Care Center to go to work in the Community Center. But when she hadn't returned to get him after normal work hours that day, he was simply gone.

Her stomach cramped with anxiety but she forced a smile of gratitude as June set a cup of steaming coffee in front of her. "How many people are staying here?" she asked as she waited for the coffee to cool a little bit.

"We have between eight and ten people at any one time," June said as she broke a couple eggs into a small bowl. "The numbers are constantly in flux, but right now we have Darcy, sometimes here and sometimes at her new boyfriend's. And then there's Lacy Matthews and her three-year-old twins and, of course, Micah."

"I see," Olivia said.

"And also there's Jesse Grainger."

June's cheeks pinkened slightly as she poured the eggs into an awaiting skillet. "Jesse was beaten and left for dead in the woods a month ago. His brother is one of Samuel's followers and he's hoping to be able to get him out of town, but Jesse has to be careful because Samuel assumes he's dead." There was something in June's voice when she said Jesse's name that indicated to Olivia that he might just be more to her than a man she had rescued from death.

"I know Lacy," Olivia said. "She works at the Cold Plains Coffee Shop. I often went in there to get a cup of coffee on my way to work at the Community Center."

"She finally decided to take her girls and run. Samuel was pressing to make the coffee shop a place that wouldn't serve anyone who wasn't a Devotee and Lacy was determined that anyone who came in was welcome to buy a coffee whether they followed Samuel's teachings or not," June explained.

By this time June was finished making Olivia her eggs and toast and Sam was using his sippy cup to drink a glass of milk. They fell silent for a few minutes and Olivia once again found herself going back in time, terrified by how close she'd come to falling completely and irrevocably beneath Samuel's spell.

If she hadn't seen Samuel murder that man with her own eyes, then perhaps today would have been the day she got her official tattoo on her hip, proclaiming her a true believer in Samuel and the philosophies he espoused. She would have turned a deaf ear to all the whispers about unsavory things going on in the town, like so many of Samuel's other true believers.

All she'd ever wanted was a place where she felt like she belonged and she'd thought she'd found it in Cold Plains, but she'd been sucked into the vortex of an evil storm named Samuel. The only thing she could focus on now was the fact that she and Sam had escaped, but she'd been forced to leave behind her precious Ethan.

She wrapped her fingers around the warmth of the coffee mug in an effort to combat the icy chill that threatened to shiver through her as she thought of her son. Hopefully Samuel hadn't seen her. She had no idea what anyone in town would think about her sudden disappearance, but surely somebody was taking good care of Ethan.

She had to believe that to be true and she had to figure out a way to somehow get him back where he belonged, in the safety of her loving arms.

As she finished her breakfast, Darcy entered the kitchen and bid them all good morning. As Olivia got a good look at the young, pretty woman, she was startled to realize that Darcy had a lot of the same features as Micah and Samuel. Of course her bright blue eyes were in opposition to their green ones, but she had the same cast to her chin, the same strong, bold features.

Maybe Olivia was just imagining things, dreading whatever it was that Micah thought they had to talk about. She didn't want to think about the deep betrayal she felt where Samuel was concerned. She didn't want to discuss building a case against him. All she wanted was to get her son back and figure out where her life went from here.

When she had finished eating, she carried her dishes to the sink and washed them as June explained that most of their water came through a filtering system from the creek that ran nearby. Electricity was provided by either solar energy or a generator that they preferred not to run unless absolutely necessary. Throughout many of the rooms, they depended on oil lanterns and candles to conserve energy.

As Micah sauntered into the room, a spark of energy surged up inside her and she couldn't tell if it was positive or negative. There had been no man in her life since long before Sam's birth. Maybe it was only natural that she'd respond to a hot male who had brought her to safety.

She walked over to Sam, who raised his arms to be lifted from the high chair. As she pulled him out, he snuggled against her chest with a happy sigh.

"You want to take a walk with me?" Micah asked, his gaze enigmatic.

"Okay." She tried to ignore the pound of her heart as she followed him out of the kitchen. She reminded herself she had nothing to fear from him. He'd found her in the forest and brought her here to safety. He'd given her no real reason not to trust him…at least not yet.

Still her distrust of men in general ran deep. It had begun with her absent father, a man she had never known, and continued with Jeff Winfry, the man who had fathered Sam and Ethan. He'd promised to love her, to marry her and settle down as a family. She'd met him just after her mother's death and even though she'd known he wasn't Mr. Perfect, she'd believed herself in love.

There had been no settling down. Jeff had dragged

her and the children from one small town to another, working odd jobs that barely kept them fed and finally he'd dumped her and the kids just outside of Cold Plains, telling her his future just didn't include a family. Her father, Jeff and then Samuel. She was determined not to give her trust so easily again.

Micah Grayson was just as formidable from the back as he was from the front, she thought as she followed him. His shoulders were broad, his hips slim and she had to hurry to keep up with his long-legged gait.

She gasped in surprise as he opened a door and they stepped outside into the bright sunshine. They were in a small clearing filled with a babbling brook on one side and a healthy looking vegetable and herb garden on the other.

"What a beautiful place," she exclaimed.

He nodded and motioned her to a fallen tree trunk that had been fashioned into a bench. "According to June, they try to be as self-sustaining as possible here. So, she grows what she can and depends on some of us to provide the other necessities from neighboring towns."

She sat next to him on the bench and placed Sam on the grass at her feet where he immediately became enchanted with a leaf that had fallen from one of the nearby trees.

"Aren't you all afraid somebody might see this place?" she asked.

Micah shook his head, his dark hair gleaming in the sunshine. "We're sitting in a small valley between two mountains." He pointed to the jagged edge of the range that surrounded them. "The only way to get here is through the cave and you saw last night how difficult it was to find."

Although they sat several inches apart, despite the scent of the fresh herbs in the air, she could smell him, that woodsy, clean male scent that curled a ball of tension in her stomach.

"What was it you wanted to talk to me about?" she asked, eager to get this conversation over with and away from the man who seemed to both draw her and scare her just a little bit.

"I had your story checked out by a friend of mine, Hawk, the FBI agent. One of many trying to build a case against Samuel for the murders of those five women, among other things." He stretched his long legs out before him, appearing to be completely at ease.

"And what did he discover?" In contrast, she was a bundle of nerves and wanted to curl into herself to escape everything that had happened in the past two days.

"That you are what you say you are." His green eyes drifted downward, making her suddenly far too conscious of how tightly her borrowed T-shirt pulled across her breasts. She hunched her shoulders forward slightly.

His gaze lingered there for just a second and then snapped back up to meet her eyes. "You worked as a secretary in the Community Center, meaning you obviously worked closely with Samuel. You might have some valuable information that could help all of us."

"So, basically what you're saying is that you would like me to help you and your FBI friends." She held his gaze intently. "I'll do whatever I can to help you if you'll get my son out of Cold Plains and back safely here with me. But, until that happens, I have nothing more to say to you."

His stare grew harder, colder but she refused to look away. If he wanted to use her, then she had no qualms about using him first.

Samuel Grayson stood at the window in the large meeting room in the Community Center where an hour before he'd finished one of his nightly seminars. Although he'd given a rousing speech about love of community and building good lives here, the crowd had been smaller than usual and the sales of the healing tonic water after the meeting had been pathetic.

You're losing control, a little voice whispered inside his head. "No," he said aloud. It was just growing pains and the result of the investigation he knew was taking place. People were on edge because of the FBI presence in and around town, and that meant he'd just have to work harder to assure them that he had things under control.

Dammit, he'd thought he'd removed any danger to himself and his plans when he'd sent Dax Roberts, one of his most trusted men, to kill his brother. He'd known that if Micah had caught word of the investigations into the murders he wouldn't be able to keep his nose out of things. It had been easier to take him out before he became a problem.

Unfortunately, he knew he was under investigation for the murders of those women. He knew there were people in his own town working against him and it was getting more and more difficult to tell who could and couldn't be trusted.

His remaining henchmen—those not already in jail—had been working overtime, taking out the people who were overtly working against him, those who had taken a path in direct opposition of him.

He felt as if the walls of the town were slowly closing in on him and he didn't like it. He didn't like it one bit. He'd worked too hard and too long to be brought down by anyone. This was his town and he deserved all the power and money that had come along with it. He wasn't going to let anyone take it away from him.

He turned from the window, and as he walked out of the meeting room, he paused and stared at the desk where Olivia Conner usually sat.

Yet another mystery, he thought. She'd simply vanished into thin air, leaving behind one of her children. He had no idea what had happened to her, had no idea if she was dead or alive. He'd put the child with the other one, hidden away in a secured location until he could find out what had happened to Olivia.

He'd had a couple of his men check her house and they had reported back that nothing seemed to be missing—no clothes and no baby items. There had been a Crock-Pot plugged in with what appeared to be Swiss steak charred to a crisp. They'd unplugged the pot but had touched nothing else.

It was possible she'd been grabbed off the street by the FBI because of her position at the Community Center. The joke would be on them. She knew nothing except how to schedule therapy sessions for him with the locals or renting out the space in the basement that was used for weddings and celebrations.

They'd get nothing from her that could harm him. She'd been simply the office help, although he'd been close to turning her completely, and once that happened he wouldn't have minded a little intimate time with her. She'd been a hot little number despite her two brats.

Whatever had happened to her, it had appeared she'd had every intention of returning home the day that she had disappeared. If he didn't hear from her soon, he would make the appropriate plans for Ethan. He would fetch a lot of money, a handsome little boy in perfect health. Just this thought alone made him feel more in control.

He was going to be fine. The people against him would eventually drift away and he would continue his work here in Cold Plains. He wouldn't be satisfied until everyone in town sported the small *D* tattoo on their hip that marked them as his.

Chapter 3

By six o'clock that afternoon, Micah realized they didn't have enough diapers for Sam. "I feel terrible," Olivia said as several of them sat at the table. "I have a huge box at home, but I never got a chance to go back there and grab anything before I took off."

"Not a problem," Micah said. "I'll sneak into town tonight to your house and grab whatever it is you need."

June gasped. "Micah, you know you'll be shot on sight."

He smiled, a mirthless gesture that didn't lighten the dark green hue of his eyes. "They'd have to see me to shoot me."

"I don't want to put anyone in danger," Olivia protested.

He hadn't seen her since their discussion that morning. Most of the time in the afternoons, Micah went to one of the darkest, smallest rooms in the cave and slept so he'd be prepared to stay up through the night when he could use the cover of darkness to explore Cold Plains.

"I've been in town after dark several times before. It shouldn't be too great a challenge to get into your house, grab some things and then get out," Micah replied.

June looked at him dubiously. "You could always drive into Laramie and pick up whatever is needed."

"That's fifty miles away," Micah replied. "Besides, I intended to go in tonight anyway and see if I can find out where they might be keeping your son. I've already put out the word to FBI agents working the case that we're looking for the whereabouts of a three-year-old. All I really need from you is a list and a location and a house key if you have it. I'd rather go in through the door than break a window that might draw unwanted attention to your place."

"As important as the diapers are, I need you to find Ethan." Her eyes were simmering pools of emotion, pools that if he wasn't careful he felt like he might fall in.

He knew nothing personal about Olivia Conner. He had no idea what had brought her to Cold Plains, what had happened to the father of her children or who she was at her core. But, what he did know was that she drew him as a woman, not as somebody to be used to further his goals.

There was something about Olivia Conner that reminded him that he was more than just a mercenary, more than a hunter seeking the source of a deadly disease named Samuel in a small town.

Something about her softness, her aura of vulnerability reminded him that he was also a thirty-eight-year-old man who had basically been alone for all of his life.

"I just don't want to be responsible for anyone getting hurt on my account," she said.

"Trust me, I have no intention of getting hurt," he replied smoothly. "Just make me a list of things you want and as soon as it gets dark, I'll go in." He got up from the table, both uncomfortable with her nearness and knowing he needed to get some sleep before night.

He decided to check in with Hawk and used his radio to call the agent. Cell phone usage was impossible amid the mountains and beneath the cave. So, old-fashioned handheld radios were still the best form of communication between the agents hiding out in the area.

Minutes later, Micah left the cave entrance and made the long trek down the narrow passageway that would eventually lead him to the forest where he'd found Olivia and Sam.

He got to the meeting place first and stood watchful, as usual listening for sounds of anyone else nearby. An unexpected bullet to the head had not only left him with killer migraines and a burning need for revenge, but also a heightened awareness of his surroundings. Never would anyone sneak up on him again.

Normally he didn't hear Hawk's approach until he was almost on top of the meeting place, but this time he heard the snap of a dried twig and the faint whisper of feet against the forest floor.

He held his gun, alarmed by the unusual noise and then relaxed only slightly as the sandy-haired, brown-eyed FBI agent appeared. He wasn't alone. Beside him was a somber-looking dark-haired man with pain-filled brown eyes.

"It's okay," Hawk said, indicating that Micah could put down his gun. Micah pointed the barrel to the ground, but didn't holster it. "This is Dr. Rafe Black and he wanted to speak to you personally."

Micah knew that Rafe and Darcy were a couple and he also knew that Rafe was one of the good guys, helping to not only bring down Samuel, but also desperately seeking the child he'd never met but was certain existed. Rafe had his own practice in town and treated anyone who needed medical attention while walking a fine line between pretending to be part of the cult and actively working against them.

"I'm looking for my son," Rafe said without preamble. "I had a photo of him, but it has mysteriously vanished. In the picture he was about three months old and he has brown hair and brown eyes like me. He'd be about nine months old now."

"I heard from Darcy that you thought he'd been found," Micah said.

Rafe nodded. "They tried to fool me by giving me somebody else's child and pretending it was my Devin, but the real father came back and reclaimed his son."

"And you're sure Devin really exists?" Micah asked. Darcy had told him that Rafe had learned about his son when Abby had called him and that he'd sent money via Western Union for her and the child. Sounded like a potential scam to Micah.

Rafe's eyes darkened. "Definitely. Abby wasn't the kind of woman to lie. Besides, if Devin didn't exist, then why did somebody in Cold Plains go to so much trouble to force a man to give up his own son to replace mine?"

"Good point," Micah conceded.

Rafe shook his head. "Devin exists and he's being hidden someplace in town. I'll pay you whatever you want to find him. I know what you do. I know that you work for a fee. You just name your price and I'll see to it that you get it the minute that Devin is in my arms."

Micah held up his hand to stop Rafe's pleas. "I'm already on the hunt for one kid and it's possible they're both being held in the same place. All I can promise is that I'll look for Devin and there's no charge. Believe me, I'm doing all this for my own satisfaction." And of course to get Olivia to cooperate with the FBI, he reminded himself.

"You know there are rumors of secret rooms in basements where the elderly and the infirm are held until they either die or can be transported far away," Rafe said. "I've done what I can to find them, but I have to be careful because I'm still trying to win people's trust. There are also rumors about an adoption scheme and my biggest fear is that, if I don't find Devin soon, he'll be lost to me forever."

His concerns echoed those of Olivia and although Micah couldn't begin to identify with the gut-wrenching grief of a parent for a missing child, he did feel a deep worry for any child that was in his brother's clutches.

"We've been searching for these hidden rooms," Hawk said, "but so far no luck."

"If they're there, I'll find them," Micah said with grim determination. After another promise to Rafe to look for his son, the three men parted ways.

Micah headed back to the safe house, knowing that two hours later the sun would be down and darkness would begin to shroud the "perfect" little town of Cold Plains.

Once he got back, he met Olivia just inside the door,

a smiling Sam in her arms. Olivia wasn't smiling. In fact, he had yet to see her smile. Her eyes were filled with worry as she handed him a list of items she'd like retrieved from her home. Then she held out a small photo. "This is Ethan. It was taken a month ago."

He examined the photo of the handsome little boy. His blond hair was neatly cut and his features were those of his mother. He had a bright smile and green eyes that looked eager to explore whatever lay ahead.

He needed to be with his mother and his brother. It was obvious that Olivia was the kind of mother Micah hadn't had, a woman with the need to protect her children, and Ethan belonged here with her.

"I don't feel good about this," she said as she also handed him a note with her address written down and a key to the door.

Micah fought the impulse to reach out and smooth the tiny furrow that had appeared between her brows. "I'm not doing anything different than I have every night since I've been here. I'm getting to be an expert at skulking around houses, trying to catch snatches of conversations, identifying the people who are with Samuel and those who are secretly working against him."

"Just be safe," she said, the words both surprising and oddly touching to him.

At that moment Sam leaned forward in his mother's arm and with his chubby hand grabbed Micah's ear. "Ear," he pronounced proudly.

An unaccustomed smile stretched Micah's lips. "Yeah, buddy, that's my ear." He gently disengaged Sam's little fingers and stepped back. "And I'm hoping the next time I see you I'll still have both my ears."

"Don't even joke like that," Olivia protested.

Suddenly he wanted to see her smile. "If I can't manage to get him diapers then we'll figure out a way to fashion waterproof leaf covers that will make him look like a baby Tarzan."

He was rewarded by a smile that whispered an evocative warmth through him. "I'm not at all sure that I'm ready to raise a jungle boy."

Just as quickly as he'd wanted her smile, he now wanted to escape it, escape her and the little boy who cast him a wide, slightly drooling grin. He'd chosen to live his life alone, trusting nobody, caring for nobody and nothing was going to change that, especially now in the midst of his battle with his brother.

"I need to prep to get out of here." He moved past her, wanting to forget the beauty of her smile, the fact that just by looking into her soft green eyes, she got to him some way that made him both uncomfortable and just a little bit excited.

An hour later he stepped out into the deepening shadows of twilight. He had an empty rucksack on his back that could carry anything Olivia might need from her home.

As he made his way soundlessly through the woods, his mind focused only on the tasks at hand. His first was to get into Olivia's house, retrieve the items she needed and then leave as quickly as possible.

He'd hide the filled rucksack and then return to town to try to find the secret rooms that had been rumored to hide the people, including the children, not fit for Samuel's vision of perfection.

Micah knew tunnels had been found and some secret rooms discovered beneath the Community Center and under the hospital clinic, but there had been no sign in those places of the children or some of the other townspeople who had vanished.

He knew that none of the FBI agents working the area had been able to get close to Samuel's house. The stately home was guarded by armed men at all times. The general consensus was that Samuel would be a fool to have any evidence inside his private abode that tied him to anything, but Micah knew how perverse his brother could be and it would be just like him to be arrogant enough to hide evidence in plain sight.

Sooner or later he intended to get into Samuel's home. It wouldn't be tonight, it might not be tomorrow, but Micah would breach the security if for no other reason than to prove that he could.

As much as Micah would like to find Olivia and Rafe's children, he'd also like to get some concrete evidence that Samuel was behind the murders of the five women, one who had once owned Micah's heart.

He couldn't get sidetracked by Olivia's soft green eyes and need for her son. He couldn't afford to forget the reason he was here: to bring down Samuel and avenge the death of the only woman he'd ever loved.

He emptied his mind as he made his way down the mountain. The crisp night air surrounded him, adding to the adrenaline pump that had begun the moment he'd left the safe house.

By the time he'd reached the outskirts of town, complete darkness had fallen. When evening came and the nightly workshop that Samuel gave was over, most people vacated the streets of Cold Plains quickly, except the men on Samuel's payroll, men seeking those who worked against Samuel.

At this time of night, Main Street looked almost magical. Even in the bright light of day, there was sheen to the storefronts and they weren't the kind of stores you'd see in most average small Wyoming towns.

In most little towns, you'd expect to see a well-worn café with mismatched glasses and silverware, a general store where items were slightly dusty on the shelves and maybe a gas station where you could still get your windows washed by a friendly attendant.

Cold Plains was a different animal altogether, thanks to Samuel. There was a health club, a book store, a fancy vegetarian restaurant and the large Community Center. The facades were clean and colorful, breathing of a prosperity that was both inviting and insidiously seductive.

Micah knew that his brother used cult psychology not only to control those who were already under his influence, but also to recruit and bring in new members who could serve him.

He demanded a zealous commitment to his beliefs, dictated how these people should think and act, plus taught that his people in Cold Plains were the special ones, chosen to build something nobody had done before him—the perfect town with a healthy, happy community.

As he entered town he clung to the deep shadows near homes. According to the address Olivia had given him, her home was located a block off what had once been called Main Street. Samuel had renamed the streets to reflect his new society with ridiculous names like Prosperity and Tranquility.

He had no idea how long Olivia had been in Cold Plains or how she could afford to rent or take out a mortgage for her own house on a secretary's salary. He wished he'd asked her more questions about her time in Cold Plains and made a mental note of ones he would ask when he eventually got back to the safe house.

He approached her small, neat beige house from the rear. She'd told him the key worked in both the front and the rear doors. There was a nice shade tree in the center of the backyard and he stood behind it, watching the house for any signs of life.

The house was dark, but that didn't mean there wasn't somebody waiting inside. Surely Samuel was curious about her disappearance. Micah wouldn't be surprised if he'd stationed a man within to either await her return or see who else might enter the premises.

He remained behind the tree trunk for several long minutes. Nothing moved, there was no indication of anyone being inside. Finally deciding to take the chance, he darted for the back door.

The key slid in smoothly and with a faint click the knob turned easily in his hand. He opened the door slowly, his gun clutched firmly in his other hand, and waited—listening for any hint of movement, a whisper of breath that would indicate anyone was in the house.

The interior held the kind of dead silence that made him believe he was all alone. He closed the door and relocked it behind him and then pulled a small flashlight from his pocket.

He knew he was in the kitchen and smelled the odor of overcooked meat. The flashlight beam caught the white Crock-Pot on the counter and a lift of the lid let him know it was the source of the smell. Somebody had unplugged it which let him know that someone had been in the house since Olivia's disappearance.

He flashed the light around the kitchen, unsurprised to find the front of the refrigerator cluttered with displayed artwork that could only belong to a fanciful, happy three-year-old. There were landscapes with bright yellow suns and big green trees. A four-legged creature Micah suspected was a dog smiled in front of a bright red little house.

Not willing to spend more time than necessary inside, he quickly moved to the living room. It was a nice-sized room, with a beige sofa covered in multicolored throw pillows. A rug matching the colors of the pillows sat beneath a wooden coffee table and an entertainment center held a small television and an array of children's books and puzzles.

There were three bedrooms. The first one belonged to the missing Ethan. It was decorated in navy blue. Games, more puzzles and books were neatly stacked on a bookcase. Micah opened several drawers and pulled out underpants, jeans and a couple T-shirts then thrust them into his rucksack. If he managed to get the kid back, then Ethan would need some clothing besides whatever he might be wearing.

From there he moved to the next room, which was Sam's. He found the big box of diapers in the closet and jammed them all into his bag, along with a couple of tiny long-sleeved shirts and long pants.

Finally he went into Olivia's room. Although she had asked for nothing for herself, he knew she'd come to the safe house with only the clothes on her back. And there was a part of him that recognized if he had to see her in those too-tight borrowed T-shirts any longer he'd go mad.

Her room was distinctly female with a pale pink

bedspread and a vase full of fake flowers ' ι light and dark pinks on one of the nightstands.

Inside one drawer he found a stack of multicolored bikini panties and he tossed a half-dozen pair into his rucksack, trying not to think of how they might fit across her slender hips and rounded butt. He then moved to her closet where he pulled T-shirts off hangers and grabbed an extra pair of jeans.

By this time the rucksack was full and he knew it was time to get out of the house before somebody inadvertently caught the shine of his flashlight and came to investigate.

At the last minute as he was about to walk out of her bedroom, he spied a bottle of perfume on the top of the dresser. He picked it up and sniffed it, recognizing it as the faint scent he'd noticed on her the night he'd found her. On impulse he threw it into his bag, not wanting to examine the reason for his action.

He left the house the way he'd entered, through the back door. With the weight of the rucksack tugging on his shoulders, he headed for the woods. He'd drop the baggage in a safe location to be retrieved later and then head again into town to see what he could find.

He picked a huge bush in the backyard of a house nearest his escape route into the mountains to hide the bag and then went to the streets.

He knew there was a long tunnel that ran beneath the Community Center and eventually led into a utility closet inside the building. The story was that the tunnel had been built over a hundred years ago to avoid Indian raids. Micah had wondered if perhaps this would be Samuel's escape route if he found himself boxed in.

As far as he knew Samuel didn't know that the

tunnel had been found by the agents, but he couldn't be sure what Samuel knew and didn't know.

But finding that tunnel had led Micah to wonder what else might lay underground—and all things seemed to start and stop at the Community Center, Samuel's magnificent building in honor of himself. Was it possible they had missed a second tunnel?

The building was a huge structure of concrete and marble with thick columns rising up and darkened windows that allowed people to see out but nobody to see inside.

An old church bell hung high above, rung to announce unexpected town meetings and the nightly workshops that Samuel insisted his people attend.

His people. Micah frowned as he clung to the shadows and worked his way around the back of the building. The Devotees got the tattoo on the hip to mark them as his own. But Micah also knew that Samuel had to know he could no longer trust his own tattoos, that some of the people who sported them had turned on Samuel, or were working undercover.

The Community Center was the true lair of the beast, the place where Samuel brainwashed people. This is where he brought the outcasts and made them feel a sense of belonging. This is where he preyed upon their weaknesses to make them his and he was good at taking the disenfranchised and giving them hope and a false sense of power.

Micah couldn't help but believe, if there were more secret rooms, then they existed in this place, in the very heart of Samuel's work.

There were no building plans on file anywhere in the town, no way to know exactly what secrets the building might contain. But, knowing his brother, Micah had a feeling that Samuel would take a perverse pleasure in holding meetings in the large room inside, throwing parties in the basement and having captive children and ill people in secret rooms right below.

Unfortunately, those working undercover in town and those working covertly on the fringes of town had been unable to find a way in or out that might hint of any other secret rooms.

Samuel's henchmen made sure that nobody wandered around in the building that was considered the very heart of the community.

If anyone would know anything about secret passageways or rooms, surely Olivia would have heard something considering the fact that she'd worked in the building five days a week as a secretary. He definitely needed to pick her brain when he got back to the cave. And maybe it would be easier if she was wearing one of her own T-shirts and hadn't sprayed on the fragrance that dizzied his senses just a bit.

If he listened closely, he could hear the sound of the bubbling creek that ran just beyond the Center. The creek was what had brought Samuel to Cold Plains, the creek with its rumored mysterious properties that healed all kinds of ailments. According to what he'd heard, Samuel had more than a cottage industry going in bottling and selling the water.

He'd begun by forcing his Devotees to buy the liquid at twenty-five dollars a pop and the latest rumors had it that Samuel was expanding the business and exporting the bottles to distributors out of town. Selling miracles from creek water, that's what Samuel did. He was like an illusionist who could take the ugly and make it magical.

Micah moved around the side of the building but stopped and froze, slamming his back against the cool concrete as he spied Chief of Police Bo Fargo and Dax Roberts talking beneath a nearby streetlamp.

Micah hated the tall, muscular, dark-haired man who had put a bullet through his head, but he also held a pure disgust for the balding, husky man who had taken an oath to protect the town and who had become one of the most dangerous men in the area. Hell had a special place for Chief of Police Bo Fargo.

Micah also knew that if either of them caught sight of him, they'd shoot to kill. Of course it might take Dax Roberts a minute to get over the fact that Micah wasn't a ghost, considering he believed he'd killed Micah months ago.

He wished he could get close enough to hear what they were saying, what plot they might be hatching on Samuel's behalf, but they were too far away for him to make out their actual words. But he was also afraid that any movement at all on his part might draw their attention to him.

As long as they remained where they were, Micah was trapped with his back against the building, hoping neither one of them happened to glance his way.

He should have looked before he moved around the corner but now he was helpless until they moved away. He wasn't arrogant enough to believe that he could take out both of them without being shot himself.

Minutes ticked by and still the two men lingered, occasionally laughing. The sound of Dax's laughter drove a stake through Micah's heart and his finger itched to kill the man who had tried and nearly succeeded in killing him.

But he couldn't take care of that particular piece of unfinished business right now. There were too many other things that needed to be done before he could pay back Dax for what he'd done and moving a single muscle now would be a deadly mistake. He had to sit tight and wait.

His tension increased and a sense of panic started to sweep over him as bright spots began to dance before his eyes. He closed his eyes in an attempt to banish them, but when he opened his eyes again they reappeared. Auras.

A bad sign.

A very bad sign.

Crap, not now. He closed his eyes once again, attempting to will away what he knew would follow. The migraines had been a curse left behind by the bullet to his head and the last thing he needed was for one to appear at this moment.

However, the flashing-light auras continued and always preceded a particularly bad one. He figured he had about thirty minutes before he'd be brought to his knees with the most excruciating pain he'd ever experienced.

Already he felt the side of his head starting to throb. If he didn't manage to get out of this situation soon there was no way they wouldn't know of his presence.

There was no way he wouldn't be dead.

Chapter 4

Olivia paced between her room and the kitchen as she waited for Micah to return. She'd put Sam down for the night hours ago and it had been that long since Micah had left to go into town. With each minute that passed, Olivia got more and more nervous, although June tried to allay her fears by reminding her that Micah was an intelligent man, a skilled mercenary who wouldn't take unnecessary risks with his life for a couple diapers.

Still, she would never forgive herself if something happened to Micah because of her. She didn't want to be responsible for his safety. She just wanted him to get back here safe and sound, with or without diapers.

Olivia had no idea what the dynamics were between Samuel and Micah but wondered how two brothers who were fraternal twins could be so different, could be at such odds. It was obvious that Micah's goal was to take down his brother and it was just as obvious that

Samuel needed to be taken down. How had two brothers become so different at the very core? What had the Grayson family dynamics been like that had produced the two men?

The place was quiet, the other women and children having gone to sleep and the men either in the woods on security duty near the entrance of the cave or out foraging in the woods to see what might lurk there, keeping danger away from the safe house.

Never had Olivia felt so alone, and in the silence, in the utter loneliness, her thoughts turned to Ethan and she felt as if her heart was being ripped from her chest.

She should have never left without him. Somehow she should have pulled it together, hidden out until Samuel had left and then searched for her missing son. If only she'd done that, then the three of them would all be here together.

Instead she'd panicked and left her precious boy behind and if something happened to him, if she never saw him alive and well again, she'd never, ever be able to forgive herself.

She'd had a sorry excuse for a mother and she'd always vowed that she would be the kind of mother she'd longed for when she had children of her own. Jeff had certainly been a mistake in her life, but Sam and Ethan had been like two little miracles she'd been gifted with to make up for a crummy youth.

She finally stopped her nervous walking and sank down on the edge of the mattress in the small room where she'd slept the night before.

The oil lamp flickered and created dancing shadows on the walls. Was somebody feeding Ethan? Did whoever had him know that he was afraid of the dark?

That she always kept a night-light burning in his bedroom? Was somebody kissing his forehead at night before he fell asleep, waylaying his fears and wishing him happy dreams?

The idea of him alone in a room, in the dark and scared shot an excruciating pain through the very center of her. She squeezed her eyes shut to staunch a flood of useless tears.

If only she knew for sure if Samuel had seen her when he'd killed that man. If he hadn't seen her, then she might take a chance and go back to town with some wild story to explain her absence. She'd get Ethan and then leave town forever.

But if he'd seen her and she returned, she knew not only would she be lost but both of her boys would be, as well. Samuel would never allow them to leave the town alive knowing that she had information that could potentially get him arrested.

She jumped off the bed with a gasp of surprise as Micah staggered into the room. He dropped the rucksack to the floor and leaned weakly against the wall, his face blanched of all color.

"Micah, are you all right?" she asked in alarm.

"Headache." His deep voice was faint as he reached up and placed a palm against the left side of his head. "Migraine."

She grabbed him by the arm and led him to the bed where he collapsed on his back, his eyes closed as he pressed both hands to each side of his head, as if trying to keep his skull together.

He said nothing and she stood next to the bed trying to think of something she could do to help him. She knew that making noise by talking to him would probably only make it worse.

He needed quiet and as much darkness as possible and he had both with just the faint flicker of the oil lamp lighting the space.

She left the room and hurried to the kitchen where she grabbed a clean dishcloth and ran it under cold water. Her mother used to have migraines, although they were usually after a night of too much booze. Even as a little girl, Olivia could remember ministering her mother in the mornings with a cool cloth on her head.

She hurried back to Micah and found him in the same position where she'd left him. He dwarfed the double mattress, but the pain that sharpened his features, that tightened all of his muscles, made her hurt for him.

She carefully lowered herself on the edge of the mattress next to his head. He squinted open one eye and winced in pain. "I have a cool cloth," she explained softly. "It might feel good across your forehead."

He closed his eye once again and dropped his arms to his side, allowing her to tend to him. She placed the cloth across his forehead and gently ran her fingers back and forth across the cool cotton.

Immediately his muscles began to relax and he released a deep sigh. After a few minutes had passed, she knew the cloth had warmed with the contact from his fevered brow and she flipped it over and once again moved her fingers slowly, smoothly over the cloth, hoping that the gentle massage might be helping.

She felt the tension ebbing out of him, his body relaxing into the mattress and before long she realized he'd fallen asleep.

She stopped her massaging and removed the cloth

and leaned back and stared at the man sprawled on her bed. How often did he get the migraines? Had something specific happened that had brought this one on? She felt responsible for his pain, that somehow by sending him into her home she'd given him too much stress.

As she sat there, a weary exhaustion played through her. It had to be at least two or three in the morning. She didn't want to disturb Micah, but she also couldn't stay up for the rest of the night and had no idea where else to go to sleep.

There was just enough room on the edge of the bed for her to stretch out without bothering the sleeping, wounded warrior who had carried in a rucksack of diapers for her son.

She placed the cloth on the table next to the oil lantern and then tentatively lay down next to him, not touching him in any way and closed her eyes. She could smell him. The wild scent of the night and the forest clung to him, a pleasant scent that filled her head with an odd comfort.

She must have fallen asleep for when she awakened again she found Micah spooned around her back, one of his arms flung around her as if to keep her trapped against his warm, firm body.

Her internal clock told her she hadn't been asleep for just a few minutes, but rather a couple hours. Still, it was early enough she heard no morning wake-up cry from Sam.

The cave was utterly timeless, with no sunlight to allow anyone to know if it was day or night. At least she had her wristwatch but at the moment it was on the nightstand and she wasn't inclined to move a single muscle.

She figured it was probably around four or five in the morning. She also knew she should roll away from Micah, somehow extract herself from their intimate position, but she didn't move. She scarcely breathed.

He felt warm and strong and utterly male and she felt herself responding in a way that was completely inappropriate and yet she remained in place, her heart beating way too fast.

For just this single moment in time, she felt more safe than she'd ever felt in her life…in the arms of a virtual stranger. How pathetic was that? How well that spoke of the choices she had made so far in her life, choices that had led her to a man who'd left her alone with one child and pregnant with the other, and then to another man who was a cold-blooded killer among other things.

She had no idea who Micah was beneath his skin. She didn't know what forces drove him or what demons he might be battling. She only knew that there was a solidness about him that called to all the insecurities inside her. There was a directness to his gaze that made her believe she could trust him despite all the reasons she might have not to.

But you're just a pawn to him, a tiny voice whispered inside her head. *You're simply a tool to help him bring down the brother he hates.* And she would do well to remember that fact.

"Are you awake?" His deep voice was a soft, heated whisper against her neck.

For a brief instant she thought about not responding, pretending to be still asleep so she wouldn't have to move away from him. But instead she whispered yes, a bit guilty that she hadn't moved the moment she'd first awakened. As he raised his arm from around her, she rolled over to face him. "How's your head?"

"Better, thanks." He made no move to get off the mattress and so she remained where she was, warmed by the heat that radiated outward from his firmly muscled body.

"Do you get migraines often?" she asked. She liked the way he looked in the faint glow of the lantern, his features relaxed in a way she hadn't seen them before, making him look not as daunting and less like his brother.

"I didn't start getting them until five months ago after my brother sent one of his hit men, Dax Roberts, to put a bullet in my head. Unfortunately, he succeeded."

Horror swept through her at his words. How could a man be evil enough to send anyone to try to kill his own brother? And Samuel was the man she'd believed was going to help her build the life she'd always dreamed about. She'd been so deluded.

"Fortunately, it didn't kill me," Micah continued. "But, it did put me in a coma for three months. Eventually I got back on my feet and the only lingering issue is the occasional migraine."

She eyed him curiously. "What happened to Samuel? I mean, what made him the way he is…so dangerous?" she asked.

He leaned up on one elbow and reached out to push away a strand of her hair from her face. The soft touch shot a flare of heat in the pit of her stomach. He dropped his hand between them and released a deep sigh.

"We could have a long discussion about nature versus nurture. Our father was a brutal man who beat both of us on a regular basis, that is, when he wasn't beating our mother. But, from the time we were young kids, I knew there was something off about Samuel."

A frown tugged across his forehead. "He was a quiet kid, always watching, observing people around him. When we were young kids, he had no friends and seemed quite content to be alone."

"The two of you were never close?" she asked.

Tension rolled off him. "No, never. I realized early on that he was an evil little boy. Anything that was important to me, he broke or stole. Any friendships I tried to have, he'd ruin in one way or another. He liked torturing stray animals. I'd wake up sometimes in the middle of the night and find him standing next to my bed just staring at me." He hesitated a moment and then added, "He scared me more than my father." He released a rusty laugh. "I've never admitted that to anyone before."

She wanted to reach out and touch him, to assure him that his secret was safe with her. She wanted to hold the child he had been and tell him he was safe and nobody, not his father or his brother, could ever harm him.

"My old man and his beatings were pretty predictable. I could tell by the sound of the weight of his footsteps on the wooden porch when he got home after work if it was going to be a night of beatings. I knew when he drank he was always a mean drunk. I learned fairly early how to recognize the danger signs when it came to my father and avoid him whenever possible."

"A child should never have to learn to recognize danger signs in their father," she replied. "What about your mother?" Olivia knew in her heart and soul that she would never be able to stay with any man if he raised

a hand to her or her children. She'd rather be homeless and alone than allow any man to harm her babies.

"My mother was a timid woman who rarely spoke
and seemed too weary for the world all my life. She
died of heart failure when Samuel and I were seven-
teen. I think she willed herself to death because it was
the only way she had the courage to leave my father."

"I'm so sorry," she whispered and this time followed
through on her need to touch him in some way. She covered his hand on the mattress between them with one
of her own. "So, you said that Samuel scared you more
than your father did," she said, wanting to understand
the dynamics that had created a Micah, the same dynamics that had also created a Samuel.

"Like I said, my dad's rages were predictable. But
Samuel was a different kind of animal." His eyes narrowed slightly. "He was impossible to read, and even
when he displayed appropriate emotions it felt forced to
me, like he was mimicking how he'd seen others react
in the same circumstances. As far as I'm concerned,
he's a narcissist without a soul, a sociopath with illu-
sions of grandeur and he really started coming into his
own in high school."

"What do you mean?" Her heart lurched a bit as
he turned his hand to encase hers. This all felt so intimate…the semidarkness, the early hour, his touch
and the secret of his past that he was sharing with her.

"It was as if, when he got into high school, he'd
honed all the skills he needed to manipulate and fool
people. He recognized weaknesses in others and ex-
ploited them." His hand tightened on hers and his eyes
seemed to transform from forest green to black with
his memories.

"There was only one person I ever really cared about in my life. She was my high school sweetheart, Johanna Tate. She was pretty much everything to me, but on prom night I went to the bathroom and I came back to find that she was gone, along with my brother. He took her away from me that night and she never spoke to me again. She became his. She's one of the five women we believe Samuel has killed. She's one of the reasons I'm here now. I want to avenge her death and I want to make sure my brother never has a chance to create a Cold Plains again, to hurt anyone else ever again."

He withdrew his hand from hers and sat up. "Now, tell me how you came to be in Cold Plains and exactly how close you were to the devil before I found you in the woods."

There was a sudden hint of steel in his voice that made her realize he'd withdrawn into himself and she had now gone from a friendly face who'd heard his confessions to a suspect in the breadth of a heartbeat.

She sat up as well, both of them sitting Indian style and facing each other. She wanted to meet him eye-to-eye as she told him her story and she had no intention of mincing the truth. "I grew up in a trailer park in Oklahoma with a sickly, alcoholic mother. I had no friends and no place I felt I really belonged." She told him this not to gain any sympathy but merely as a statement of fact.

"My mother died when I was twenty-two and six months after that I met Jeff Winfry. He was basically a drifter, living out of a camper on the back of his pickup. He was handsome and charming and was making his way toward California with grand schemes for his future. I bought into him and his silly dreams and before I knew it, I'd sold my mother's trailer and hitched my star to Jeff."

She swallowed against the self-disgust that rose up in the back of her throat as she thought of the incredibly stupid choices she'd made so far in her life.

"Soon after that I got pregnant with Ethan." Her voice broke as she spoke the name of her missing child. "Jeff kept telling me we were going to get married and settle down someplace and like a stupid fool, I believed him as we went through small town after small town. In each place he'd work side jobs for cash and made me believe he was checking it out to see if the area was good enough to settle down with a family, but he rejected each town and we'd move on."

She frowned, remembering her feeling of helplessness, of hopelessness and the self-recriminations that had filled her with each day that passed.

"When I was six months pregnant with Sam, we hit Cold Plains. Jeff pulled up next to a bench along the sidewalk on Main Street and told me that he'd realized he really wasn't cut out to be a family man, that Ethan and I were cramping his style. He left us there with a suitcase full of clothes and a hundred dollar bill and then he drove away."

She could still remember the utter terror that had consumed her at that moment. She was six-months' pregnant and with a two-year-old, abandoned in a strange new town where she knew absolutely nobody.

"Did you love him?" Micah asked.

She didn't answer immediately, but instead took the time to really think about it, about Jeff. "I thought I was in love when I left Oklahoma with him, but I realize now that I was really in love with the idea of escaping the place that had been such an unhappy home, I loved the idea of an adventure with a man who I thought loved me. And then once I got pregnant with Ethan, I thought I loved him because he was the father of my baby and I wanted to build a family. But, now I recognize that it wasn't love that drove me, but rather need, the need to belong to something…to someone." She released a humorless laugh. "God, I sound so pathetic."

"No, you sound human," he countered with a gentle tone. "When I was eighteen, I joined the navy for the same reason. I needed a place where I felt like I belonged. I was a Navy SEAL for five years before I went out on my own. You've probably heard I'm a mercenary. I take money to get rid of problems that our government doesn't want to touch." He studied her, as if waiting for a negative reaction.

She was in no position to judge anyone for the choices they had made in their lives. Besides, she didn't care what he'd done in the past. All that mattered was that he was here now to take down his brother and hopefully help her get her son back.

"So, you were dumped in Cold Plains. What happened next?" he asked.

"I was still sitting on the bench crying when, a half an hour later, Samuel found me. He got me to tell him what had happened and he was so kind to me. He told me not to worry, that I'd landed in the right place where people would help me get on my feet and that he could teach me how to live a healthy, happy and productive life in a wonderful town."

She felt the burn of tears in her eyes as she thought of how easily she'd allowed herself to fall under Samuel's spell. "He was so soothing, so persuasive and he immediately took control of the situation. He led me to a small furnished house where he said we could stay for the time being. Several men brought in food and then Samuel told me about his workshops, that there was one that night and I should attend. I did and I almost immediately bought into everything he proselytized. He gave me my job and allowed me to remain in the house." She felt the warmth of heat in her cheeks. "I even named Sam after him."

"A perfect town where there's no crime, no illness, no drug or alcohol abuse. A perfect town where everyone is healthy and happy and a leader who is willing to work and see that come to fruition, of course you bought into it. You were all alone and afraid, a perfect victim for my brother."

"I was a fool," Olivia replied with a touch of anger. "I gave up my free will, took the job he offered me, lived where he told me to live and didn't even think about doing anything to break one of his many rules. I was ready to get a tattoo to show my devotion to him when I saw him shoot that poor man. In that single moment, it was like I woke up from a dream and realized I'd given up everything I had to him. I gave my mind, my heart, my very soul, to a cold-blooded murderer." She fought against a chilly shiver that threatened to run up her spine.

"And that's when you ran," Micah said.

She gave him a curt nod. "At first it was sheer panic. I needed to think. I needed to process what I'd just seen. I felt as if the world had suddenly shifted and I couldn't hold my balance. I ran for the woods and hid."

"Do you know the identity of the man he shot?"

She shook her head. "It was too dark for me to see who it was. There was just enough streetlight shining for me to see Samuel, but I couldn't make out who was with him."

"And you don't know if Samuel saw you or not when he killed that man?"

"If I knew for sure he hadn't seen me, then I would have gotten Ethan before I ran." She couldn't stop the emotion that welled up in her chest, pressing tight and making it nearly impossible for her to draw a breath.

Hot tears began to streak down her cheeks. "Once I'd run to the edge of town and into the woods, I was afraid to leave Ethan, but I was more afraid to go back into town. I figured if Samuel had seen me, then I'd put Sam at risk as well as Ethan if I went back."

She was unable to stop the tears as her emotions careened further out of control as she thought of her little boy. Like the migraine that had brought Micah to his knees, the pain inside her nearly incapacitated her.

Shoving a hand to her mouth in an attempt to staunch the cry of pain that thoughts of Ethan brought, she looked at Micah helplessly.

She knew she was falling apart from the inside out and he seemed to sense it, too. He knelt and pulled her up to her knees, then wrapped his arms around her as she began to shiver with the fear she'd scarcely allowed herself to feel when she thought of her absent son.

If not for his arms around her, she'd shatter. If not for his strong thighs against her own, she'd explode into a million pieces, so great was her sense of loss at that moment.

She almost believed she was going to be able to re-gain control, she almost had herself convinced that she was strong enough to step away from the dark abyss that called to her, and then he gently caressed her back.

"Let it go," he said softly in her ear. "Just let it all go."

As he gave her permission, the grief that had ripped at her very soul since the moment she'd left Ethan behind overwhelmed her. Weakly she leaned into him, allowing her tears to fall in earnest as deep, gulping sobs began to escape her.

Flashes of memories shot off in her head. Ethan gazing up at her proudly as he completed one of his puzzles. His blond hair shining in the sunlight; his laughter riding the breeze as he tried to catch a ladybug; he'd been her heart since the moment of his birth.

Each memory only made her cry harder. Micah didn't say another word, but he tightened his arms around her and continued to move his hand up and down her back in a soothing fashion.

He didn't seem uncomfortable with her display of emotion, at least she didn't sense any uneasiness. Instead there was simple acceptance and, in that acceptance, a comfort she knew she wouldn't find anywhere else.

Finally her tears slowed and then stopped and still she remained in Micah's embrace, slowly becoming aware of the faint scent of shaving cream that lingered on the underside of his jaw, the taut muscles of his shoulders beneath her fingertips and the slow, steady beat of his heart against her own fluttering heartbeat.

Within moments her heartbeat mirrored his, slow and steady as she felt the last of her sad emotion ebb away and a new one begin to take its place.

She couldn't ever remember feeling so good in a

man's arms and as he reached up and stroked the length of her hair, she felt the quickened beat of his heart.

Suddenly she felt less safe than she had moments before. A faint sense of danger simmered through her, a danger that wasn't all unpleasant, but rather whispered of delicious undertones.

She was leery of trusting anyone in her current situation and given her bad history, but Micah called to something inside her. But she couldn't allow herself to let down her guard in a moment of an emotional outburst.

She pulled back from him enough that their bodies no longer touched. "Sorry about that," she said as she swiped at her cheeks.

"No need to apologize," he replied, his eyes dark and glittering in the faint light. "Sorry about this."

She looked at him curiously just before he wrapped one of his hands around the back of her head and pulled her toward him. She had no time to process, no time to deny him as his mouth took possession of hers.

The kiss torched fire through her entire body and despite the fact that she hadn't been prepared for it, that didn't stop her from responding completely. She opened her mouth to welcome it, to welcome him, and his tongue tasted of hunger as it danced with hers.

When he finally released her, she stared at him, appalled that she wanted more, that something about Micah Grayson touched her like no man had ever before in her life.

"I'll find your son," he said, his eyes still glittering like a wild animal's trapped in the faint illumination. "No matter what it takes, no matter who I have to go through to get him, I promise I'll find your son for you and bring him home, no strings attached." His voice rang with a conviction that made her believe him.

His gaze softened and she thought he was going to kiss her again but, at that moment, Sam hollered from the room next door, his cry of Mama echoing through the cave.

"Thank you," Olivia said as she got off the bed, her head still reeling from the kiss they'd shared. As she left the room, she tried to prepare herself for another day in hiding, another day without her beloved Ethan and attempted not to think about what might have happened if Sam hadn't awakened at that very moment.

Chapter 5

Micah sat in the kitchen alone, half-irritated by his promise to Olivia. He didn't make promises—to anyone, ever—and yet he'd made one to a blond-haired, green-eyed woman who had somehow managed to get under his skin. Not just with the haunting sadness in her eyes, not just with the sobs she'd been unable to control, but also with the story she'd told him about who she was and where she'd come from.

She'd never had a chance in hell against a man like Samuel. She'd been a victim ripe for the picking, already kicked around by life. He was only surprised that Samuel hadn't tried to take things further with her, make her one of his very special girlfriends. Of course, that probably wouldn't have happened until Samuel personally tattooed the *D* on her hip, marking her as his forever.

Micah wrapped his hands around the coffee mug,

the thought of his brother touching Olivia making him half-sick. Thank God Olivia had gotten out when she had. It was just unfortunate that she'd had to run before grabbing her son.

It was midafternoon. Breakfast had come and gone and everyone in the house was busy with duties or whatever.

After Sam woke up, Micah had left Olivia's room and gone to his own quiet small space where all he'd been able to think about was the kiss he'd shared with Olivia. He was shocked to realize he somehow wanted to be the hero she'd never had in her life, the man she could depend on to get her son back, to make her world right.

If Sam hadn't awakened when he did, Micah had a feeling the sexual attraction between him and Olivia might have spiraled completely out of control. It had been a long time since he'd been with a woman, an even longer time that he'd been with a woman whose name he'd remembered after having meaningless sex with her. He wasn't proud of that, it was simply a part of his life he hadn't thought much about.

Once he'd lost Johanna to Samuel something had broken inside him, the part of his heart that allowed people in, the part that allowed him to trust. He'd decided at that time that he would live his life alone, and up until now he'd never regretted that decision.

His sole goal when he'd arrived here was to pay back his brother for the bullet to his head, for the migraines that sometimes brought him to his knees and for the death of the woman he'd believed he'd once loved.

Now he'd made a promise to a woman he couldn't seem to get out of his head, a woman whose kiss had fired a flame inside the pit of his stomach that still hadn't stopped burning.

Despite all the reasons he shouldn't, he trusted her. He believed her story and he also believed her new-found horror of Samuel. Samuel might have been able to "turn" her at one time, but Micah knew there was no way she could be corrupted by Samuel again.

She wanted her kid back and then they'd figure out a place for her to go where she could start a new life and this time learn to stand on her own two feet. He sensed a deep core of strength inside her. All she had to do was tap into it and she and her kids would be just fine.

He'd finally fallen asleep and had awakened just a few minutes before, long enough to pour himself a cup of coffee and sit at the table to think about options for finding Ethan and Rafe's little boy, Devin.

He looked up as Darcy Craven entered the kitchen. She paused at the sight of him, as if considering running out of the room. Since the moment he'd met her, she seemed to be avoiding him and that, coupled with a strange sense of familiarity about her, intrigued him.

"Darcy, why don't you sit and have a cup of coffee with me?"

"Okay," she said with a faint touch of reluctance.

He watched as she got a cup and filled it with the brew. Darcy was young, probably no older than twenty-two or twenty-three, but she gave the aura of an older, more mature woman.

She sat across from him at the table and he noted her long, dark hair and bright blue eyes. Was it her eyes that made him feel the odd sense of familiarity? Or the shape of her face? She definitely reminded him of a woman he'd known years ago, but if he thought about it, she could remind him of lots of women he'd known through the years.

"I met your fiancé. He's asked me to look for his son," Micah said.

"He's frantic to find him." Her blue eyes flashed with the fire of anger. "It was wicked for somebody to give him a little boy and tell him the child was Devin and then have the baby ripped away from him by the true biological father."

Micah nodded. "So, what's your story? I'm still trying to figure out who is who and all the connections between Samuel, Cold Plains and everything else."

Darcy looked down into her coffee cup, as if considering how much or how little to share with him. "A few months ago I discovered that the woman who raised me, Louise Craven, wasn't my real mother. As Louise was dying, she told me that I'd been left with her by my biological mother who feared for my life. Louise told me she was haunted by my mother who seemed to vanish into thin air and now that I was an adult it was time I searched for her and become the family we were meant to be."

"No leads at all?" Micah asked, still studying her features intently.

"Ford McCall, he's one of the local cops and one of the good guys, showed me a picture of one of the dead women, one who is a Jane Doe. He seemed to think I looked like her, but really the only resemblance was that we both have blue eyes. I don't know if she's my mother or not."

"Do you have the picture?" Micah was aware that one of the five murder victims was listed as an unidentified Jane Doe, but he hadn't had any contact with

Ford McCall, one of the few law enforcement officers in town who was working on their side, or seen whatever picture the man might possess.

"No, but I can get a copy from him." She took a sip of her coffee. "I just want to find out who my mother is, whether she's alive or dead and why she left me with Louise when I was a baby. Louise told me my mother grew up as a foster child in a small town. I found out she was from the small town of Horn's Gulf and I went there and showed the photo around but nobody could tell me if she was the foster girl who lived in town for a short period of time."

"Horn's Gulf. That's where I'm from," Micah replied in surprise.

"I know." She frowned and in that gesture a rivulet of shock shot through Micah.

The shape of her face, the dark hair...the frowning gesture that he'd seen not only in his own mirror on occasion but also on his brother's face. Was he just imagining the resemblance?

"What about your father?" he asked with a forced nonchalance, although his heart suddenly beat an unsteady cadence.

Once again, Darcy looked down into her coffee mug, as if unwilling to meet his eyes. "What about him?" she countered in a faint whisper.

"He's Samuel. Samuel is your father, isn't he?" Micah felt as if his heart had stopped beating in his chest.

Darcy's blue eyes looked miserable as she met his gaze. "There was a note pinned to my pajamas the night my mother left me with Louise. It said 'keep my precious baby safe from Samuel. Never let her know the truth.' But, before she died Louise told me the truth, that my father was a dangerous man named Samuel Grayson who was running a cult in Cold Plains. That's what brought me here in search of my mother."

She paused to take a sip of her coffee and he noticed her hand tremble slightly as she set the cup back down on the table. "I came here and forced myself to go to some of Samuel's seminars. I made friends with some of the Devotees, all the while trying to find out any information about my mother that I could, but nobody was talking. I got a job working as a receptionist in Rafe's office and I finally told him the truth about my father. Rafe knows, and June knows, and now you know, too, and I hate it. I hate that he's my father," she said fervently.

"But that makes you my niece," Micah replied, the new information rolling around in his head.

A tentative smile curved her lips. "And I haven't decided yet if that's a good thing or a bad thing."

An unexpected burst of laughter left Micah's lips and he wasn't sure who was more surprised by the spontaneous response, he or she. "I hope given some time we'll both decide it's a good thing."

"Time will definitely tell," she said, meeting his gaze boldly now.

A sense of respect swept through him for the young woman…his niece. She'd come into the lion's den seeking answers about her mother, answers that so far hadn't been forthcoming.

She would be a fool to trust him completely, knowing him for only a couple days and knowing that he was Samuel's brother.

A surprising swell of emotion rose up in his chest.

He had no family except for Samuel. There had been no aunts and uncles, no cousins, only a nervous mother who had escaped a brutal man five years before he'd met his own death in a drunk-driving accident.

Micah had never thought much about having a family. He'd certainly never felt any family love or support when growing up on the small ranch in Horn's Gulf.

His mother had been distant, his father had inspired fear rather than love and he'd written off his sick brother when they'd been young kids.

When he'd arrived here at the safe house, he hadn't expected to find a niece, nor had he expected to find a woman like Olivia. He wasn't sure how to handle the whole thing.

He hated the fact that Olivia had seen him at his very weakest, so sick with his vicious headache the night before. When the two men standing beneath the streetlamp had finally parted, Micah's head had reached full pound mode.

He was both nauseous and weak as he'd made his way back to retrieve the rucksack and continued on to the safe house. He'd barely managed to make it to safety.

"Are you okay?" Darcy's voice pulled him from the moment of the night before when he had feared his headache would ultimately be the death of him.

"I'm fine, just trying to digest everything that I've learned in the week that I've been here."

"All you really have to remember is that when meeting people from Cold Plains, you can't trust anyone other than the people Hawk introduces you to or the ones June has vetted." She took another sip of her coffee and then carefully set the cup on the table. "I just want to find my mother."

Her blue eyes filled with emotion. "I'd hoped to find her alive, to be able to build a relationship with her, but I think she might be dead. I think she might be the Jane Doe that Ford has been trying to identify. Unfortunately, until he identifies her with her name, I won't know if she's my mother. Louise told me my mother's name was Catherine, but that's all I know."

Micah frowned. "Catherine George. That's who you reminded me of the night I first saw you in the woods. I think I called you that."

Darcy leaned forward. "That must have been after I fainted at the sight of you." When Micah had stumbled into Darcy and June in the forest the first time they'd met, Darcy had assumed he was Samuel and had dropped into a dead faint. "Catherine George? Was she in Horn's Gulf?"

"Yes, but there were several Catherines in our school. To be honest, I didn't pay much attention to the girls who flocked around Samuel, but the moment I saw you I thought of her." He shrugged. "And now I see myself and Samuel in your features, but your eyes still kind of remind me of Catherine George. Maybe it's just because they're so blue. I wouldn't take that name to the bank. It's possible Catherine George is alive and well and never had a daughter she gave up to protect. You get that picture from Ford and I'll take a look at it and maybe I can make a definite identification."

She flashed him a grateful smile and then stood. "Thanks." She paused for a moment. "You know, you might look a lot like Samuel, but you're really nothing like him."

"That's the best compliment you could give me," he replied. She nodded and left the kitchen, leaving Micah alone with his thoughts. There were times when he was haunted by the possibility that he was more like Samuel than he wanted to admit.

He'd worked as a mercenary, infiltrating for the sole reason of taking out a life. He'd fooled men and women, pretending to be something he wasn't, focused solely on what he'd been paid to do.

Did that make him like his brother? Were they both narcissistic power seekers who simply used different methods to achieve their goals?

Disturbed by his own thoughts, he got up from the table and carried his and Darcy's cups to the sink where he washed them out and set them on a drainer to dry, then went in search of Olivia—telling himself he needed to pick her brain about everything she knew about the Community Center—but in the depths of his heart he suspected he just wanted to see her beautiful, sweet smile to erase the doubts about himself he'd just entertained.

Olivia had learned soon upon arrival at the safe house that it was located in Hidden Valley, and her favorite place to spend time was in the secret garden where the sun shone down and Sam could play in the last of the late summer grass.

Besides, she felt like they needed the sunshine to keep their internal clocks set right. It would be easy in the cave to lose track of day and night and she wanted to know exactly how many days she'd been without her baby Ethan.

At the moment she was seated next to June, who

had been sharing with her the trauma of nearly dying a month before when two of Samuel's henchmen had managed to infiltrate the safe house. Nearby, Jesse Grainger, a rancher from the Wind Rivers foothills, walked the rows of vegetables, giving the two women a chance to talk alone.

Initially it had been June who had saved Jesse's life when she'd found him half-dead and suffering from amnesia in the forest. But on the night of the attack, it had been Jesse who had saved June's life and in the process he'd won her heart.

One of the infiltrators had been killed and the other had been taken away by the FBI, leaving the location of the safe house a secret.

Sam sat at their feet, his attention divided between the sippy cup of juice he clutched in his chubby hand and Eager, the black Lab that lay dozing at June's feet.

"Sooner or later Sam's going to make a grab for Eager," Olivia said as she watched her son sizing up the big dog.

"Eager is very tolerant of people and children as long as I don't have his work leash on him," June replied. Eager was a search and rescue dog who June often took with her to the woods to help hunt for people in trouble—or people trying to cause trouble.

The warmth of the mid-September sunshine on Olivia's face was welcoming and yet she couldn't help but wonder if Ethan was enjoying the sunshine. Was he someplace swinging or playing in a sandbox, enjoying the last of summer with other children his age? Or was he locked up in some room with an armed guard as a playmate?

"Micah promised me last night that he'd get my son out of Cold Plains," she said to June.

"He strikes me as a man who doesn't make promises easily," June replied with a touch of obvious surprise.

"I just hope Ethan is still in town." Olivia swallowed hard against the lump that had risen in her throat. "You know there have been those rumors of illegal adoption activity."

June nodded. "That's Rafe and Darcy's biggest fear for his son, that he's already been adopted out to somebody and they'll never be able to find him."

"If that happens to Ethan then I'll spend the rest of my life looking for him. Surely when Samuel is eventually brought down, the FBI will find paperwork or something that will name a baby broker, somebody who will be a lead to where the children went." She tried to tamp down the anxiety that threatened to take hold of her.

But a different kind of anxiety filled her as Micah stepped outside. Every nerve in her body hummed at the sight of him. Instead of wearing the camouflage clothing she'd been accustomed to seeing him in, he wore a pair of jeans that hugged his slim hips and a long-sleeved navy polo shirt that stretched across his broad shoulders and muscled chest. He was clean-shaven and the scent of minty soap clung to him.

He looked sexy and rugged and utterly capable of accomplishing anything he put his mind to. He smiled as he approached and her heart fluttered, the memory of those sensual lips pressed against her own heating her insides.

"Nice day to be out here," he said as June stood from the bench where she and Olivia had been seated.

"Unusually warm for this time of year," June replied. "Won't be long and it will be too cold to sit out here. I hate to think about the snow falling." She looked from Micah to Olivia and smiled. "I think I'll head inside and get started on something for dinner." As she moved toward the door, Jesse gave a nod to Micah and Olivia, and then, along with Eager, they all disappeared back inside.

"Mind if I sit?" he asked and gestured to the place next to her on the bench.

"Of course not," she replied, although she couldn't halt the rapid race of her heart at his nearness. "I want to thank you for all the things you got from my house." She'd been delighted when she'd opened the rucksack earlier and had discovered not only diapers, but also clothes for both her boys and for herself.

"I figured your life was in a big enough uproar that at least you should have some of your own things to make you feel better."

She rubbed her hands down the thighs of her well-worn, comfortable jeans. "I definitely feel better in my own clothes." The long-sleeved cotton red blouse she wore didn't tug across her breasts and made her less self-conscious than she had been in the borrowed things. And she couldn't believe he'd thought to throw in the bottle of her favorite perfume.

"I want to pick your brain about the Community Center," he said.

"What about it?" she asked in surprise.

"I believe that somewhere in that building are the secret rooms we're searching for, that it might be the place where Samuel is holding both Rafe's son and yours. It's just a gut feeling, but I want you to tell me about every room, every doorway you know of in the building."

"Why do you think there are any more secret rooms there?"

Micah's eyes narrowed slightly and, with the cast of the sun on his lean face, he looked more like his brother than ever before. "Because Samuel is a sadist and I think he'd get off on the idea of having his nightly seminars with all his people gathered in the auditorium and not knowing that some of their loved ones are locked up right beneath where they stand."

He shrugged. "I'm just trying to get into his head, to think the way he'd think."

"Try not to do too much of that," she said drily. "I think his head is a very dangerous place to be."

He smiled and in the warmth of that gesture all semblance of Samuel fell away. Samuel smiled often, pretending to be a loving father figure, a benevolent leader who wanted nothing but good for the town and its people. But she realized now that when Samuel smiled, no real warmth danced in the depths of his eyes.

"There really isn't a lot to the Community Center. Samuel has an office there, where he spends most of his time during the days and the evenings. I sat in the reception area. There are a couple small rooms that are used for more intimate counseling, and then there's the auditorium where he holds his town meetings and seminars."

"What about storage closets?"

"There are three that I know of," she replied thoughtfully. "But somebody told me they'd already found a tunnel beneath the Community Center that led out of one of the closets."

Micah nodded. "I can't help thinking if there's one tunnel then there could possibly be another one, leading to another place inside the building. I know the one that was found is thought to be an old settler tunnel used as a hiding place from marauding Indians, and I assume Samuel might intend to use that as an escape route if he ever needs to. It leads partway up the mountain, but he isn't the type to leave himself only one option for escape."

Sam reached out and grabbed Micah's knees and pulled himself up to his feet. Micah looked surprised as Sam gave him one of his most charming grins.

"Sorry," Olivia said and reached out to grab her son. Micah lifted a hand to stop her. "He's fine."

Sam slapped him on the knee and laughed, as if agreeing with Micah that he was just fine. A small smile curved the corners of Micah's lips. "He doesn't seem to have many trust issues," he observed.

Olivia smiled ruefully. "He's never met a stranger he didn't like. Children are born pure and trusting. They have to be taught not to trust. Unfortunately they learn too early that people aren't always what they seem, that promises are rarely kept and that sweet unadulterated trust they're born with is broken."

She should have learned her lesson about trusting men when she'd been old enough to realize her father had abandoned her and her mother when she was just a baby.

"Have you ever been in Samuel's house?"

She blinked at the question that came out of nowhere. "A couple times, mostly just long enough to step into his foyer to deliver or pick up paperwork. But, last year he gave a big Christmas party there and invited all the people who work for him. Why?"

"According to what Hawk told me, they haven't been able to get anyone inside. They have no grounds for a warrant and it's guarded at all times. Not even any of the men who are working undercover have managed to get through the front door. What's it like on the inside?"

Sam sat back down on the ground, apparently bored by the adult conversation. He made no move to crawl away. Sam was pretty much content wherever he found himself. It was Ethan who had been her little explorer, always crawling or running with her chasing after him.

"Olivia?" Micah's voice pulled her back and she looked at him.

"Samuel's house is beautiful. I'm sure you already know it's in an area of town with huge houses and yards that abut the mountains. Inside, there's a large foyer with a grand staircase that leads to the next floor, although nobody went upstairs the night of the party. The party was held in the great room, and it is magnificent with a stone fireplace and a wet bar and a wall full of sliding doors that lead out to a balcony. The house is built on a rise, so when you walk in you're actually on a second floor."

"Selling tonic water must be lucrative," Micah said drily.

Olivia grinned ruefully at him. "Oh, Samuel gets money from much more than just the tonic water. We pay to attend his workshops. If he suggests private therapy then that's another expense. I imagine he probably gets a kickback from all the businesses in town."

"Yeah, that's what we figure, but according to Hawk they've been unable to gather enough evidence of anything to get Samuel behind bars. He's played things very safe and close to his vest. Even some of his devoted worker bees that we've managed to gather up won't turn on him."

Olivia leaned back thoughtfully and raised her face to the sun, needing the warmth to fill her soul as she went back to the night she'd seen Samuel kill a man.

She finally returned her gaze to Micah. "You know, even if I go to the FBI and tell them what I saw Samuel do, it's only my word against his and I'm sure he'll have half a dozen people who will alibi him for that time on that night. I honestly don't think my statement would move your investigation any further along and, at the moment, all it would do is put my son at greater risk."

Micah raked a hand down his lean, handsome features. "And we don't want that to happen." He released a deep sigh. "As much as I hate to admit it, I think you're right. If it comes down to your word against Samuel's, he'll be pulling alibi witnesses out of his ears."

"There's a lot of fear in that town. People are afraid to speak up against your brother," she said.

They fell silent, the only sound the song of a bird in a nearby tree and Sam patting the ground like it was a drum. For Olivia it was a tense silence as her mind refused to stop playing the kiss they'd shared through her head.

She couldn't stop thinking about the way it had felt to be held in his arms. She also couldn't help but worry about him. It was obvious he was determined to take down Samuel at all costs. Hopefully in the process he'd find her son and reunite her with him.

But, in the meantime, she knew the danger he faced each time he got near Cold Plains. She understood that those nights when he crept beneath the cover of darkness into the streets of Samuel's paradise, the risk of him losing his life was very real.

Definitely her trust in him grew by the minute, especially after he'd shared so much personal information with her. But she didn't want to care about him. She didn't want her heart to somehow get tangled up in his.

There was a battle brewing, a battle of epic proportions. What frightened her more than anything was the fact that there was no way of knowing which brother would remain standing when the war was won.

Chapter 6

As Micah and Hawk moved through the forest toward the small cabin where three FBI agents were hiding out, Micah couldn't get Olivia and her children out of his head. When Sam had pulled himself up using Micah's legs as support and given Micah that wide grin, something soft had risen up inside Micah, something he hadn't known he possessed.

The last thing he wanted at this moment was to embrace anything soft that might be hidden on the inside. He needed to be tough. He needed to be strong and single-minded for what lay ahead.

Get Ethan and Devin out of town and take down Samuel. Avenge Johanna's death and cut the evil cancer from the earth forever. It was like a constant mantra in his head as he moved behind Hawk toward the meeting place.

Still, it was hard to stay tough, and not to allow some

of the softness he'd discovered to seep to the surface whenever he was around Olivia.

It had been a week since he'd found her crouched in the bushes and had taken her to the safe house. In the last couple days, she had seamlessly fit into the group, offering to help whenever possible and building a special relationship with Darcy because of the two missing children.

He'd spent a lot of the last week with her, talking not just about the Cold Plains and Samuel, but also about her life with her alcoholic mother and her desire for something so much more, something so much better for her own children.

It was only after Sam had gone to bed, when the night was full upon them that he saw the despair creeping into her eyes, that he watched the slight tremble of her hands as she realized yet another night was about to pass with Ethan still gone from her arms.

When she finally went to her room, he fought the impulse to go with her, to hold her and comfort her, because he feared that comfort would lead to another kiss and a kiss would lead to something far more than either one of them needed in their lives at this time.

He was here with a single purpose and when that goal was accomplished he had no idea what the future held for him, but he was certain it wasn't a fragile blonde with two fatherless children.

They were in the very depth of the forest now and Micah knew Hawk was as tense as he was as utter darkness folded in around them. Scurrying noises indicated furry creatures shunning their human presence in the wild domain that should have belonged only to them.

Micah knew the difference between the natural

sounds of the forest and the alien sounds of hunters and he knew Hawk could discern the difference, as well.

Each man carried a penlight to shine on the faint, overgrown path they followed. Although they would prefer to move with no light at all, it was impossible as not even a sliver of moonlight penetrated the wildness that surrounded them.

Some of the tension that had ridden Micah's shoulders eased as he spied a faint light flicker in the distance. The cabin. Hawk had told him there were three FBI agents holed up there, coordinating the investigation, and Micah was anxious to talk to them, to kick around ideas for making some sort of forward progress.

He felt as if everything had stalled out, and each time he saw that sadness that shadowed Olivia's beautiful eyes, his need to do something to break the case wide open grew more intense.

Hawk halted abruptly and Micah nearly back-ended him. The agent took a radio from his pocket and warned the men in the cabin that he was coming in with one.

From the outside the cabin appeared to be an abandoned hunter's hideaway. The rough wood of the small place blended perfectly into the tall trees that huddled against it.

As the two men approached, a flash of light shone at a window, there a moment and then gone. It was only when the door opened that a light spilled onto the forest floor and then quickly disappeared as the door slammed shut behind Hawk and Micah.

In the first instant of being inside the cabin, Micah was eternally grateful that he wasn't one of the three men sharing the small space. Before the introductions between the men were made, Micah felt more than a faint touch of claustrophobia building up inside him.

Boyd Patterson, Stephen Jeffers and Lawrence Rosenbloom all had the wild eyes and vibrating energy of men cooped up in a small space for too long. They greeted Micah and Hawk with the friendliness of long-lost relatives, obviously eager for somebody's company besides their own.

They gathered around a wooden table that took up the center of the room. Three cots lined the walls and a small cookstove and sink took up what was left of the cabin.

"Pretty stark conditions," Micah said as he eased down across from Boyd.

"Hey, at least we have a bathroom with running water. Things could be worse," Lawrence said.

"You really do look like him," Stephen observed, his gaze intense on Micah.

Micah nodded and reached up to touch a length of his long hair. "The major difference is at the moment Samuel is working his movie star persona and I'm sporting more of a homeless look."

Stephen cast him a wry grin. "I hope that's not the real major difference between yourself and your brother. Still the resemblance is really remarkable."

Just that quickly the conversation turned serious as Micah began to tell the agents about the Samuel he'd known as a child, the Samuel who had appeared to come into his own during high school and the man who was now the charismatic leader of the "perfect" people in the "perfect" town of Cold Plains.

"I still don't know all the players," Micah said. "Hawk has been trying to fill me in, but there's a lot going on in town. I do know that two children are missing and one of my personal priorities is to find them and return them where they belong."

Boyd nodded. "Rafe Black's baby and Olivia Conner's son. We're aware of the situation and we have agents attempting to find the location of the children, but so far with no success."

"People are afraid to talk even if they aren't a part of Samuel's nonsense. Their fear of reprisal from him is too high," Lawrence said.

Stephen leaned forward. "What we were hoping you could give us is some idea of any weaknesses that your brother might possess, some quality that we can exploit to our advantage."

Micah frowned. "I've stayed up nights trying to figure out a weakness Samuel possesses that can be utilized. The only real weakness is his own arrogance, but he's also highly intelligent and apparently has made few, if any, mistakes." Micah shrugged. "I'm not sure anything I know about him can help you."

Micah didn't even consider mentioning to these men that Darcy Craven was his brother's daughter. There was absolutely no way Micah wanted her used somehow as leverage even if it meant losing the war. He would not allow his newly found niece to be collateral damage in the battle against Samuel.

"We've been keeping track of the traffic in and out of town and, if it's any relief at all, we believe the children have not been transported from the area," Boyd said.

"Has anyone managed to get inside Samuel's house?" Micah asked.

"None of our people, but we've spoken to some who have been inside. We've surveyed the area around the house and have found nothing suspicious. But without a warrant, our hands are pretty well tied. Why?" Boyd's gaze was as intense as the other three on Micah.

"We know about the secret passageway beneath the Community Center. I assume Samuel probably figures that's an escape route for him if anything goes down there and he needs to get out. I can't imagine him not having another from his home," Micah replied.

Stephen nodded. "We've thought the same thing, but the house is guarded 24-7 and we can't find a way to get inside legally, and of course officially we can't go in illegally."

"You can't, but I can," Micah countered. "I don't have to cut through red tape or follow anyone's rules. I don't work for the FBI."

"Yeah, but to get into that house, you've got to go through big burly men carrying big burly guns," Lawrence said.

Micah recalled what Olivia had told him about the wall of sliding glass doors that led out to a balcony. "Maybe...or maybe I can find a way around them."

Hawk's eyes narrowed. "What are you talking about?"

"Don't worry about it," Micah replied, deciding the fewer people who knew his plans the better. "Now, tell me exactly where we are in the investigations into the murders."

It was a little over an hour later when Hawk and Micah finally left the cabin. They moved silently through the forest until they reached the place where they normally met to speak to one another.

"Are you heading back to the safe house?" Hawk asked.

"No. I'm heading into town. It's relatively early and Samuel should be in the middle of one of his nightly brainwashing sessions," Micah replied.

He needed action. A restless adrenaline surged up inside him. He needed to do something to break this all wide open. For Olivia. For Darcy. And for every vulnerable person in Cold Plains and the entire state of Wyoming or wherever Samuel might decide to set up a new kingdom.

"Don't do anything stupid," Hawk said softly. "We still need you alive and working on our side of this thing. You're a vital piece of this operation."

"Trust me, I plan on being around until the bitter end. I'll check in with you tomorrow," Micah said as he turned and headed toward town.

He knew that almost every night at eight o'clock Samuel gave his seminars and demanded that most of the townspeople attended. If anyone was going to get inside Samuel's house and explore, the best time would be during the seminars when Samuel was busy "teaching" his flock.

Micah had no intention of trying to get inside tonight. He'd need the right equipment to play spider and get up to the balcony. He didn't have time to get the hook and rope he'd use from the safe house and then return to town and take care of business before Samuel ended his nightly meeting.

Tonight was strictly a reconnaissance mission, to see the lay of the land around his brother's house and find out how many guards were on the place.

Although he'd been in the area almost two weeks, he had stayed away from Samuel's home, instead focusing on checking out the Community Center and learning the positions and names of all the players in this deadly game.

It was difficult to be thrust into the middle of an operation where you couldn't be sure who to trust, where the enemy could come at you with a smiling face and a knife tucked behind his back.

He'd had months of catch-up to accomplish, thanks to the bullet to his head. But now he was ready to truly begin the hunt, both for the missing children and the key to bringing down Samuel's kingdom.

As he headed into Cold Plains, his thoughts went to the victims that they were certain had been killed by Samuel or at the very least at his bidding.

Shelby Jackson had been found five years ago in Gully, Wyoming, a mere five miles away from Cold Plains. She'd been twenty-nine, single and rumored to have been dating Samuel at the time of her disappearance. Hers had been a cold case until the other victims had begun showing up.

The second victim was the Jane Doe that Darcy suspected might be her long-lost mother. Her body had been found four years ago and she'd had a tiny temporary black *D* written with a Sharpie pen on her right hip. It was possible she'd been attempting to pull herself off as a Devotee without getting the actual tattoo, perhaps working undercover.

Victim number three had been Laurel Pierce, found three years ago. She'd been dating Jonathon Miller, a personal trainer at Cold Plains Fitness, which was owned by Samuel. Miller had been cleared of any connection with her death.

Abby Michaels had been a new teacher's aide at Cold Plains Day Care Center, the mother of the missing

Devin. Her body had been found in the Laramie area, fifty miles away from Cold Plains, a few days before the fifth body was found.

And finally there was Johanna Tate, found on April 2, almost six months ago. It had been the report of her body being found that he'd watched in that coffee shop in Kansas, along with a fresh-faced reporter indicating that her body was one of five all tied to the small town of Cold Plains and a man named Samuel Grayson.

In the moments immediately following the newscast, a myriad of emotions had crashed through Micah. A grief like he'd never known before, coupled with a killing rage directed at his brother, nearly brought him to his knees.

He'd paid for his coffee, stepped out of the coffee shop and had immediately put in a call to the FBI, deciding at that moment that he would join their fight to bring down the brother who he knew was evil at his very core.

It had taken only hours before Micah got a call from Hawk Bledsoe, the agent in charge of the investigation. They had planned a place and a time to meet the next day. And that night Micah had gotten into his car to drive to a café for some supper and before he could start his car engine, Dax had appeared at the side of his car.

"Your brother says hello," he'd said as he'd shot Micah through the head.

Micah stopped in his tracks, drawing a series of deep steadying breaths as he fought against the memories of the past. He'd had no idea how Samuel had found him in that small town. According to the doctors and nurses it had been nothing short of a miracle that he'd survived the gunshot at all, especially without any signs of brain damage.

There was nothing he could do now about the months he'd lost in the coma. There was also nothing that could be done to save Johanna. All he wanted now was to somehow save Olivia by finding her son and in the process get whatever information he could to see to it that Samuel was destroyed.

As usual when he entered the town, he moved through the backyards of houses, using trees and brush and whatever else was available to hide his presence.

When he got close enough to the Community Center, he moved closer to the street where he saw cars and trucks parked in front, attesting to the fact that Samuel's nightly gathering was still ongoing.

A slight nausea welled up inside him as he thought of Samuel preaching to his flock, filling their heads with the kind of cult programming that stole away the ability to think for oneself. If he listened carefully, it was possible he would hear chanting coming from the building, the chanting by rote that altered the way people viewed their surroundings, the entire world. Us against them, that was the message Samuel would deliver on a regular basis. Us against the rest of the world. He'd use those words to work on building paranoia and allegiance to his cause.

The still-in-progress meeting would definitely make it easier for Micah to check out his brother's house. Despite the guards he'd been told were always on duty around the mansion, he wanted to get as close as possible to survey the landscape around the structure, to see if getting onto the balcony and in through the sliding glass doors that Olivia had described was a viable option.

Samuel's neighborhood was one of the newer upscale areas that had appeared in the small town. Micah had heard the house next to Samuel's had been built by a successful actress who used the place as a vacation home when she wanted to escape the stress of Hollywood.

Micah wasn't sure who the other neighbor was, but it was a no-brainer that whoever it was was wealthy and influential and had bought into Samuel's fantasy of life in this particular small town.

Thankfully the houses were built on two-acre plots that were covered in trees, making it easy for Micah to keep his cover as he advanced closer to Samuel's place.

He stopped behind a large tree when he had the house in sight. Just as Olivia had said, it was an impressive structure and from his vantage point he could easily see the balcony that ran the length of the place, a balcony that could be reached with a simple grappling hook and rope.

He tensed as he saw a large man with a rifle slung over his shoulder walk around the back of the house. *One of the guards,* Micah thought. He wondered vaguely how Samuel justified armed guards on his home in a town where he professed there wasn't any crime.

The guard looked bored; he walked the perimeter at the rear of the residence without casting a single glance around the area, as if the last thing he expected was any kind of trouble.

Good. Complacent guards were far easier to take out or to get around. Still Micah remained where he was, knowing he needed to keep watch to see who else might make the rounds, see if he could get an exact number of men and how often they made the trek around the structure. He checked the illuminated dial on his watch to note the time.

As he waited, he couldn't help that his thoughts returned to Olivia. Her appearance made her seem fragile, but he knew there had to be a core of steel inside her and he found that as attractive as her aura of vulnerability.

And it wasn't just Olivia who was crawling under his skin, it was Sam, as well. The kid had definitely taken a shine to Micah and he had to admit he found the little boy both fascinating and charming.

He kept telling himself he needed to keep his distance from both her and the kid. He didn't know how to be a partner and he definitely didn't know how to be a father. He was the very last thing she needed in her life.

He was built to be alone and she needed a man who would know what normal was when he saw it. Micah had never known normal. His family had been the poster image for dysfunctional and he would never know if the parenting he and Samuel had endured was ultimately what had created a monster like his brother.

As a second man began to make the trek around the back of the house, Micah instantly recognized him as Dax Roberts. Micah glanced at his watch and realized fifteen minutes had passed since the previous guard had made the rounds.

He settled in to watch for another hour or so, wanting to make sure that the timing of the guards remained about the same. In fifteen minutes Micah could easily be up a rope and onto the balcony without anyone realizing his presence. But he had to be sure of the routine of the guards before he could chance a bold move like that.

The next hour ticked by slowly, but confirmed to Micah that the guards made the rounds every fifteen minutes or so. There appeared to be only two guards, as Dax and the other man alternated trips around the house.

After an hour had passed, Micah felt that he had the information he needed. He waited to leave until Dax had made his pass around the back of the house.

Dax was halfway around when he stopped suddenly and his head snapped in the direction of the trees where Micah hid. Micah froze, scarcely breathing. He knew he hadn't made a sound, but it was as if Dax sensed a presence…a presence that didn't belong.

Micah remained frozen, hoping he blended into the landscape perfectly. There was no way Dax had actually caught sight of him. Maybe he was just doing a general scan of the area, taking his job more seriously than the other guard had done.

Both men were frozen in time, Micah hidden and Dax hunting. Sweat trickled down Micah's back as Dax took a step toward the area where Micah was hidden.

The last thing Micah wanted was a showdown now and instinctively he took a step backward and the crisp snap of a twig beneath his foot cracked in the air.

"Who's there?" Dax's rifle was immediately ready to take aim as he began to run in the general direction of where Micah was standing.

Micah's gun was ready as well, but in an instant all kinds of scenarios flew through his head. The sound of a gunshot would bring more men and there was a possibility that Micah would never make it back to the mountain alive.

At one time he would have taken the chance, he would have shot Dax and to hell with the consequences, but he had the weight of a pair of beautiful green eyes and a promise he'd made to Olivia to consider.

If he died now, who would look for Ethan Conner and Devin Black? The FBI agents were focused on bringing down Samuel, and Micah feared that finding the kids was secondary to their ultimate goal.

Someplace in the very depths of his soul, Micah believed he was Ethan's only chance. It made no sense to feel that way, but he couldn't control what he felt in his heart. And with this thought in mind for the first time in his life, Micah ran from a fight.

He turned and didn't even bother to mask the sound of his escape. He just ran, dodging from tree to tree to avoid a bullet to his back. "Hey!" Dax shouted. "Halt."

Micah did no such thing. He crashed through the trees and then along the back of the houses, heading toward the mountain at the other end of town where he knew the terrain, where he knew he could get lost.

As he raced, he was vaguely aware of the sound of Dax chasing after him. Too much moonlight, Micah thought as he tried to keep himself from becoming a target for the shotgun.

As skilled as Micah was in subterfuge, Dax proved a worthy opponent when it came to hunting. Not only was Dax an issue, but the other guard had apparently joined the game, as well.

Micah breathed shallowly through his nose, his focus solely on getting to the mountain wilderness where hopefully he could lose both of his pursuers. Still, his heart pounded with adrenaline as he jigged and jagged through yards, around houses and behind sheds. He jumped fences and crashed through bushes, ignoring barking dogs and the flash of backyard lights blinking on.

He'd just managed to reach the woods when Dax's voice rang out from far too close behind him. "Stop or I'll shoot."

Micah felt the rifle pointed at his back and he knew Dax wouldn't have a problem pulling the trigger. The only thing he had going for him was an element of surprise. Hopefully he could use that to his advantage.

He stopped and slowly raised his hands above his head as if in surrender and then turned to face Dax. In the bright moonlight that spilled down, he saw Dax's face blanch of color and for just a moment the rifle in his hands dipped toward the ground.

Micah sprang sideways, throwing his body down to the ground and into the brush. He rolled as far as possible before rising back to his feet and running.

He'd only gained a few seconds' lead, but it was enough to momentarily lose Dax. He knew that if he ran to the left he'd be taking Dax in the general direction of the safe house. If he ran straight ahead he would eventually wind up on the cliff with no way to escape. The only choice he had was to veer right and hope he could somehow lose the man he knew would kill him if he got the opportunity.

He ran as fast as he could for several minutes given the darkness and the terrain and then stopped, slowed his breathing and listened.

He heard a faint crunch of leaves to the left of him and knew that a true cat-and-mouse game had begun.

He had two objectives. If he couldn't lose his hunters, then he could at least lead them far away from the direction of the safe house. His second objective was to find a hiding place so good, they'd eventually give up looking for him and head back to town to report to Samuel.

The moonlight created dancing shadows among the trees, and every nerve in Micah's body was on edge as he tried to move as silently as possible while keeping alert to any imminent danger.

He knew there were at least two of them and there was no way of knowing if they'd radioed for any backup. There was a strong possibility that, within minutes, the forest would be swarming with men all with one single goal in mind—to kill Micah.

And Micah didn't dare try to use his radio to summon backup. The crackle of the radio would alert anyone nearby to his whereabouts. He just couldn't take that chance. He was on his own.

He threw himself to the side, his heart skipping a beat as the rifle cracked and a piece of bark chipped off a tree nearby. His heart pumped as fast as his thoughts while his gaze darted first one direction and then the other, seeking escape.

Funny, he'd never thought much about self-survival before this moment. Throughout his years as a mercenary, he'd taken dangerous risks, aware that the outcome might ultimately be his death and that had never bothered him before.

But now he had Olivia and Sam to think about. He had two little children missing from their parents who needed him to find them. He had a niece he had just met, a young woman he already admired and would like to get to know better.

For the first time in his life he felt as if he had people depending on him, a reason for being and all he wanted to do was get out of this forest alive.

Chapter 7

Olivia awoke, her heart banging hard in her chest from the nightmare that had just jerked her from her sleep. In the dream Samuel had been chasing Ethan down the street as the little boy ran for the safety of her outstretched arms.

In the dream she'd been frozen in place, unable to do anything to help Ethan as he ran. Samuel streaked after him, his features twisted into the image of a horrendous monster.

"Run," she'd cried to her son, her heart crashing against her ribs as she fought to break the spell that held her motionless. "Run, Ethan, run to Mommy!"

She now drew a deep breath and released it slowly to calm the frantic beat of her heart. The worst part was that she'd awakened just before Ethan's little body had slammed into hers, just before she'd been able to wrap him in her arms and smell the scent of him, feel the sweet warmth of him.

Sliding her legs over the side of the bed, she decided going back to sleep would be impossible for a while. She still tasted the terror of Samuel on her tongue, still felt the weight of despair of not being able to grab Ethan away from him deep in her heart.

She threaded her fingers through her hair to smooth any sleep tangles as she made her way to the door. Maybe a cup of hot tea would soothe away the residual tang of terror, the overwhelming sense of loss that still lingered in her soul.

She opened the door, taking one step out into the hallway, and came face-to-face with Micah. It was obvious he'd just come in from the forest. Wildness was not only the scent he wore, but also what radiated from his eyes, the wildness of a man pumped up on sheer adrenaline.

"What happened?" she asked, tension instantly flooding through her.

"Nothing. Everything is fine." His words were clipped, his voice deeper than usual.

"You don't look fine. You look like you're about ready to jump out of your skin," she replied.

He stared at her for a long moment and then grabbed her by the wrist, pulled her back into her room and shut the door behind him with his foot.

She barely released a gasp as he backed her against the stone wall, leaned into her and took her mouth in a searing kiss that buckled her knees and sent her senses reeling.

The intimate contact against her let her know that he was erect and someplace in the back of her mind she knew she should push against him, halt the kiss and step away. This was dangerous.... He was dangerous, but it was a danger that called to her.

His mouth was hot and hungry against hers, as if he'd lost all control and although she had no idea what had happened to him outside tonight, his obvious need stoked a flame inside her that she allowed not just to burn slightly, but to completely explode.

She yielded to him, raising her arms and locking them around his neck as she pulled herself more tightly against him. She had no idea what had happened, could scarcely process what was happening at this very moment, but she knew whatever it was, she was going to encourage it to continue.

He finally tore his mouth from hers and leaned back, staring into her eyes as if seeking an answer to an unspoken question. The wildness was still there in the green depths of his eyes, but there was also a hint of desperate need and it was that emotion that drew her in.

She dropped her arms from around his neck and stepped back from him. His glittering eyes went flat, as if he knew he had overstepped boundaries and was now prepared for the consequences.

When she grabbed his wrist and tugged him toward the bed, his eyes glittered once again, this time with a flame that nearly stole her breath away.

Once they stood next to the bed she pulled her T-shirt over her head, just to make sure he understood her intentions. For a moment he appeared to be mesmerized by the sight of her in her plain white bra and jeans.

As he remained planted in place, she wondered if perhaps she'd misread the situation, taken it further than he'd intended for it to go. But as that thought fully formed in her mind, he pulled the long-sleeved black shirt he wore over the top of his head and tossed it to the floor.

If the kiss had simmered a flame inside her, the sight of his naked, hard-muscled chest shot desire like a wildfire through her veins. The flickering oil lamp played on the planes and contours of his bronze skin and with their gazes locked, he kicked off his shoes as his fingers went to the button of his black jeans.

This time she was the one who remained frozen in place as he took off his jeans, leaving him clad in a pair of briefs that did nothing to hide the extent of his arousal.

As he gazed at her, the wildness was still in his eyes and the energy that rolled off him filled the room, filled her. It was like being caged with a slightly dangerous animal, only she had no desire to escape, no desire to run from him.

Instead she took off her own shoes and then removed her jeans, leaving her in her bra and a pink pair of bikini panties he'd picked up for her when he'd gone into her house.

A tremble began deep inside her as he advanced toward her, his eyes gleaming with intent, with a hunger that felt as if he'd already touched every inch of her body.

When he reached her, he wrapped her in his arms and kissed her once again; she tasted his wildness in the kiss and she responded with an abandon of her own.

They fell on the bed, his mouth not leaving hers as he rolled so that she was beneath him. She knew this wasn't about lovemaking, but it didn't matter. It was about human connection, about the need to confirm that despite the chaos that surrounded them, they were both okay and still very much alive.

Still, when his lips finally left hers, he tenderly stroked her face as his eyes glittered down at her. "I want you." The words were stark, without any real emotion.

She had no idea what had happened to him tonight, but once again, despite the flatness of his tone, she sensed a need in him and it called to the same kind of emotion inside her. "You have me," she replied.

His eyes flared and he leaned to one side, allowing him to stroke down her neck, across her delicate collarbones and then capture one of her breasts through the material of her bra. Even through the cotton she could feel the heat of his touch and her nipple hardened in response.

She closed her eyes and gave herself to the sensations of his body next to hers and his hand touching her breast. It had been so long since she'd felt the quickening of her own breath with desire, the accelerated beat of her heart with sweet anticipation.

He reached behind her and unfastened her bra, then plucked it off her and tossed it to the floor at the side of the bed. His mouth replaced his hand, sucking in her bare, erect nipple and rolling it with his tongue.

A gasp of sheer pleasure escaped her lips as she grabbed hold of his hair in an effort to pull him closer… closer still. As he licked and teased first one nipple and then the other, his hands worked to remove her panties and when he got them partway down her thighs, she did the rest, removing them so that she was completely naked to him.

Within minutes he had taken off his briefs and their

touches, their caresses grew more intimate. As he moved his fingers against the center of her, she arched up to meet him as she felt the rising tension that begged to be released.

When the release came it washed over her in wave after wave, as she weakly clung to his shoulders and cried out his name.

He gave her no time to breathe, but instead took complete possession of her, sliding into her with a deep thrust. He took her hard and fast, as if exorcizing inner demons, but she didn't care. She met him thrust for thrust, releasing all her pent-up rage at Samuel, despair over Ethan and passion that Micah stirred inside her.

As the tension once again buoyed up inside her and he increased the speed of his strokes, she saw in the flickering light of the oil lamp the taut cords in his neck, the lack of control in his eyes. A second climax shuddered through her and at the same time he found his release, gasping hoarsely against her neck and then rolling from her and collapsing by her side.

For several long moments the only sound was the echo of their breathing as they waited for their heartbeats to return to normal, as they waited for their bodies to calm after the storm they'd just shared.

She finally turned over to face him, her body still tingling from his touch. "What happened to you tonight?" she asked, instinctively knowing that what had just occurred had been prompted by something.

"I just took you like a beast without any thought of birth control or anything else and you're wondering what happened to me tonight?" One of his dark brows raised as tension once again possessed his features.

"I'm on birth control shots and had my last one

less than a month ago. You don't have to worry about that. As far as you taking me like a beast, I was right there with you. No complaints from this very satisfied woman." She offered him a smile, hoping to erase some of the strain that showed on his handsome face.

He rolled over on his back and released a deep sigh. "I overplayed my hand tonight."

She leaned up on one elbow. "What do you mean?"

As he told her about scoping out Samuel's house, about being seen by Dax Roberts, fear for Micah shot through her, forcing her to recognize the growing feelings she had for him.

"I managed to lead Dax and one of the other henchmen toward the far side of the mountain and finally I lost them and came back here."

She knew there was a lot he wasn't telling her, that the chase through the forest hadn't been as easy as he'd related. She scooted closer to him as if by her close presence she could somehow protect him from the dangers outside of this room, outside of the cave.

He wrapped an arm around her and pulled her against his side. "The whole time I was running, all I could think about was that I'd made a promise to you and I had to stay alive in order to fulfill that promise," he said softly. "It's what kept me moving, what kept me from engaging into a fight."

Olivia's heart squeezed tight in her chest. "Then I'm grateful that you made me that promise," she replied, her voice thick with emotion.

"He nearly killed you before, Micah. I'm sure Dax Roberts would love to complete the job he thought he'd already done. Forget the promise you made to me. Don't go into town anymore. Leave it all to somebody else.

Hopefully the FBI working this case can find Ethan and bring him home to me."

He frowned. "I don't make promises often, but when I do, I never break them."

She reached up and stroked a hand across his furrowed forehead. "Then I release you from this one." As much as she wanted her son back, as much as she needed Ethan in her arms once again, she couldn't allow Micah to risk his own life to accomplish that feat. She moved her hand and placed it on his heart. The beat was steady and strong. "I'm afraid for you, Micah."

He covered her hand with his own. "There's no reason to be afraid. The only thing that's really changed is that now my brother knows I'm still alive."

And it was those very words that shot a shiver of fear straight through Olivia's heart.

"What is so damned important that you had to get me out of bed?" Samuel asked as he belted his silk robe more tightly around his waist. He stared at Dax Roberts who stood before him in Samuel's great room.

Dax Roberts wasn't a huge man, but he had the flat eyes of a cold-blooded snake and carried himself with an aura of suspended danger ready to break loose. Samuel knew just how dangerous Dax could be, but he'd never feared the man. Dax knew he belonged to Samuel and the man would be a fool to bite the hand that fed him, and fed him very well.

At the moment Dax's gaze refused to meet Samuel's and a hard pit of tension formed in Samuel's stomach. This could only be bad news, otherwise there was no way Dax would have awakened him in the middle of the night.

"What's happened? Spit it out, man." Impatience made the words snap from Samuel.

Finally Dax's black gaze rose to meet his. "We caught somebody skulking around the house while you were in the middle of your seminar."

"And?" The idea that somebody had been sneaking around the house didn't particularly bother Samuel. He knew the FBI were prowling around the whole town and it certainly wasn't a surprise that they would have agents slinking around his house. After all, he was their biggest target. Fortunately, they had no legal reason to get inside. That was the thing about law enforcement agencies...they had to play by the rules, but he didn't.

"And me and Larry chased him up into the mountain but we eventually lost him." Dax's eyes narrowed, as if affronted by his own failure to capture the intruder.

"And why is this important enough to wake me up?" Samuel asked, his irritation growing by the second. A threat that had vanished into the woods in the mountain was no threat now. "Couldn't this all have waited until morning?"

Dax's jaw muscles tightened. "I thought you'd want to know.... It was your brother."

Samuel stared at him, certain he must have misunderstood. "My brother? What are you talking about? My brother is dead. You killed him."

Dax frowned and his gaze shot to the floor at Samuel's feet. "Apparently he has nine lives."

The small pit of tension that had coiled in Samuel's stomach swelled outward, filling his chest with a barely contained rage. "Are you positive that's who it was?"

Dax gave a curt nod of his head. "It was him, there

was no question. I got a good look at him in the moonlight."

"So, it would seem you didn't do the job I sent you to do," Samuel said, his anger just barely controlled. Dax was lucky, for if Samuel had had his gun in his hand at the moment, Dax would be dead.

"I swear, I shot him almost point blank in the side of his head. He should be a dead man." Dax took a step backward, as if fearing the reprisal of the unsuccessful job.

Samuel balled his hands into fists at his side. "It appears you didn't complete your job. I don't like half-ass work, Dax. I expected better than that from you." Dax's eyes went flatter and the muscles in his jaw tightened. "Get out of here and don't talk to me again until the job is done correctly," Samuel said with disdain.

Dax wasted no time leaving the room. A moment later Samuel heard the sound of his front door opening and closing and it was only then Samuel allowed his rage to explode. He grabbed a nearby vase and hurled it at the fireplace, finding no relief in the splintering of glass.

Micah.

Micah was alive.

He stalked to the sliding glass doors and pulled one open, then stepped out onto the balcony and pulled his robe around him again against the cold night air. His gaze shot in the direction of the mountain looming high above in the night sky.

Someplace on that mountain the brother he thought was dead was not only breathing and alive, but was obviously actively working against him.

Samuel had spent years becoming the man he'd

become, building the skills necessary to take a small town and make it his own. He hadn't feared the fists of his father, he'd had only disgust for the woman who'd been his mother. But he'd hated the simple existence of Micah since he'd been a young boy.

He'd always felt like Micah saw through his carefully constructed facade, that somehow the fraternal twin that had shared their mother's womb with him was more like him than either of them wanted to admit.

Therefore he'd always seen Micah as a threat to all that Samuel wanted to accomplish, a potential obstacle that had to be removed.

He'd thought that had been accomplished. He'd thought Dax had taken care of the problem months ago. First thing in the morning he'd tell his men to be on the alert for Micah. He'd make sure they all knew there was a healthy bounty on Micah's head. And hopefully by this time tomorrow he'd have the body of his dead brother at his feet.

Chapter 8

Darcy awakened before dawn. She could tell it was early because there were no sounds echoing through the cave walls, no scent of early morning coffee to indicate that morning had arrived.

She leaned over to reach her wristwatch on the table by the bed and checked the time in the light from the flickering glow of the oil lamp. Just before five. June would be up within an hour or so. Most of the house came alive between six and seven.

She picked up the sheet of paper on the table and stared at the artist rendering of the victim still called Jane Doe. The woman's bright blue eyes stared back at her and long blond hair fell in soft waves down to her shoulders.

Jane Doe. Was this woman her mother? Darcy had gotten the copy of the picture from Deputy Ford McCall two days ago, but until now she'd been oddly reluctant to show it to Micah.

She desperately wanted an answer and yet was afraid of the answer she might get from him. She knew that if he recognized the woman from his hometown of Horn's Gulf, if he remembered her name had indeed been Catherine George, then that meant she was probably Darcy's birth mother and there would never be the reunion between the two that Darcy had hungered for.

She leaned back on the bed and stared at the dancing shadows on the ceiling. She didn't want her mother to be dead, killed by either Samuel Grayson or one of his henchmen. She squeezed her eyes tightly closed for a long minute, willing away the sudden press of tears.

She wanted the opportunity to embrace her mother, to ask questions that couldn't be answered by anyone else. She wanted to know all the reasons her mother had chosen to leave her behind. She needed to know if her mother had thought about her each and every day.

She wanted to see if her laughter mirrored that of her mother's, if they had the same slender fingers. She wanted to feel the connection to the woman who had given her life and then had left her in the care of another for safety's sake.

Louise Craven had been a kind and loving woman. She'd raised Darcy to have high morals and to be independent and strong. She wanted to have the opportunity to show her mother who she had become, that she was somebody to be proud of.

Darcy had become close to both Deputy Ford Mc-Call and his fiancée, Gemma Johnson. Gemma had nearly been sucked into Samuel's control when she'd come to town after being beaten by her ex-husband, a brutal man who had eventually wound up murdered.

Like Olivia, Samuel had attempted to take the broken and wounded Gemma under his wing, but ultimately Gemma had fallen in love with Ford and been saved from Samuel and the cult.

Darcy knew how committed Ford was to finding out the identity of the Jane Doe, despite the fact that Chief of Police Bo Fargo had told him to lay off. The last thing Bo Fargo wanted was the identification of another woman definitely tied to his boss, Samuel. Still, Darcy had found solace both in Ford's undeterred commitment to give a dead woman a name and in Gemma's friendship.

She'd also found solace in Rafe's arms. It was hard for her to believe that in the evil town of Cold Plains she'd managed to find a good man with a good heart who loved her as deeply as she loved him. But Rafe would never be truly happy until he got his son Devin back. It was a missing piece of his heart that Darcy couldn't fill.

Darcy was reminded of Rafe's loss each time she saw Olivia, who feared for her own missing child. Darcy's heart ached for both of them, the man she loved and the woman she now called friend. She knew what it felt like to have a missing mother, but she couldn't imagine the torture of having a missing child.

Two weeks ago she'd been working as a receptionist in Rafe's doctor's office and spending her nights next to him in his bed. But Rafe had felt things beginning to unravel in town, had sensed that danger was getting greater and greater and in a burst of macho protectiveness had insisted she come and stay here in the safe house. But that didn't stop her from occasionally sneaking back into town to spend a couple hours in Rafe's arms.

His biggest fear had been that somehow Samuel would recognize her as his daughter and use the information in some negative way to hurt her. Samuel had already shown the fact that family meant nothing to him when he'd sent a man to kill his own brother. If what Darcy believed was true, it was possible Samuel had killed her mother. What would he do if he knew she was his daughter?

Rafe had said that he would explain her absence by telling people Darcy had left town. As far as anyone knew she had no ties to Cold Plains, had simply drifted into town months earlier. There was no reason for anyone to believe she might stick around.

She missed Rafe desperately during the time they were apart, needed his arms around her when she showed Micah the picture of Jane Doe. But he was on a hunt for his son and she knew by agreeing to spend most of her time here, she'd relieved his mind as far as her own safety was concerned.

Darcy got out of bed, recognizing that going back to sleep wasn't an option. She might as well hit the shower, dress and start the morning coffee.

As she left her room she wondered how this would all end? Would Rafe find the son he believed belonged to him? Would the FBI ever be able to get the evidence they needed to finally put Samuel behind bars?

Finally, was her mother alive and well or was she the Jane Doe in the picture? Killed by one of Samuel's men and buried a hundred miles away from Cold Plains?

Micah reluctantly escaped Olivia's bed at dawn and left the room, his head still dizzied with the scent of her, the warmth of her. He would have liked to stay and make love to her again, this time with tenderness and caring instead of the adrenaline-pumped possession of the night before.

He would have liked to linger in bed, watch her wake up and then show her that he could be a different kind of lover than he'd been previously.

But he had to meet with Hawk. He had to tell the man that Micah's presence here was no longer a secret to his brother. Leaving Olivia sleeping, he grabbed his clothes from the floor and went to the bathroom where he washed up and then went into the small room he called his own. He changed into a clean pair of camo pants and a long-sleeved matching shirt and then left the room. He saw nobody in the kitchen as he passed through but noticed that the coffee was already made. Somebody besides him had crawled out of bed unusually early.

Once outside the predawn air was cold, portending of the winter to come. Winter in the mountains would be harsh and make things a hundred times more difficult for the people in the safe house. Travel would be difficult and footprints were easily followed in the snow. He hoped to hell they would all be out of here by then.

Within minutes he didn't feel the cold as he hurried through the woods toward his meeting place with Hawk. He'd radioed Hawk a few minutes before to set up the encounter.

They occasionally met later in the morning to exchange any news that might be pertinent to the case. But Micah still felt the rush of the chase last night, the concern that now his brother had the knowledge that he'd survived the attack from months earlier.

When he reached the fallen tree where he and Hawk always met, he sat on the trunk, thinking about the night before. It had felt as if the chase through the woods had taken hours…days. Several times Dax and his partner had gotten close enough to fire shots, barely missing Micah as he led the two farther and farther away from the safe house location.

When he'd finally lost them and felt safe enough to double back to the safe house he'd still been pumped up, topped off with an adrenaline rush that had him half-wild. And what had he done? Grabbed Olivia, pulled her into her room and shoved her up against the wall like some crazed animal thinking only of his own needs.

And he'd needed to rid himself of the wildness, had needed to release the adrenaline. He frowned as he realized he'd also needed…he'd wanted Olivia. And she'd willingly accepted him, met him thrust for frantic thrust, as if the madness that had momentarily gripped him had been contagious.

The whole thing bothered him, but what bothered him more than anything was the question of when he'd come to a place where he needed anyone? When had it happened that he felt he needed Olivia?

After they'd made love, he'd stayed with her, pulling her tight against him as they both had fallen into an exhausted sleep. When he'd awakened this morning she'd still been sleeping and he'd spent far too long watching the play of the oil lantern glow on her features.

The scent of her had clung to his skin as he'd left her bed without awakening her. The scent, coupled with the memory of how she'd accepted him so easily into her bed, how she'd stroked his forehead as he'd told her about what had happened in Cold Plains, had made him feel for the first time in his life that he wasn't alone.

And for all of his life, Micah had been alone. He hadn't had a family to bond with, nor had he gotten close to any of the men he'd served with while he was a Navy SEAL. As a mercenary, being close to anyone, trusting anyone, was definitely a liability.

This thing with Olivia was like nothing he'd experienced before. He hadn't wanted to leave her this morning; already he looked forward to returning to the safe house just to see her face, watch that beautiful smile curve the lips that drove him half-mad with desire.

He even liked spending time with Sam, who made him laugh with his childish antics and obviously had taken a real shine to Micah, insisting that Micah pick him up whenever they were in the same room.

He frowned and shifted positions as he wondered what was taking Hawk so long. He didn't want to think about Olivia and Sam. Last night should have never happened. Making love to Olivia had definitely been a mistake. She and Sam were complications in the life he'd chosen for himself, people who had no idea that he had nothing real to offer them long-term.

As he heard a faint rustle of leaves, he jumped up, gun drawn and then relaxed as Hawk came into view. Hawk looked like he'd just climbed out of bed, but although his sandy blond hair was askew, his brown eyes were alert and curious.

"A little early for a meet. What's up?" he asked.

"I'm no longer the FBI's dirty little secret," Micah replied.

Even in the tiny beam from his flashlight, Micah saw the frown that creased Hawk's brow. "What are you talking about?"

"I was doing a little lurking around Samuel's house last night and I was seen by the two guards. They chased me up the mountain for probably an hour or so before I finally managed to lose them."

"What makes you think either of them recognized you? I mean, when you're all cleaned and spit polished you might look like your brother, but right now I'd think it would be hard for anyone to see a resemblance."

"Unfortunately, one of the men chasing me was the same one who put the bullet into my head almost six months ago," Micah replied.

"Dax Roberts?" Micah nodded while Hawk shook his head. "That one is a particularly nasty piece of work."

Micah fought the impulse to reach up and touch his scar. "Trust me, I know."

"Are you sure he recognized you?"

"Positive. He had a rifle pointed right at my chest and if it hadn't been for a moment of his stunned surprise at seeing me alive and well, he would have put a second bullet into my body. Thankfully I used his surprise to my advantage and dropped and rolled to avoid being shot. I figure within an hour of him losing me in the forest he informed Samuel that I'm still alive."

"I'd hate to be Dax right now," Hawk said drily. "I'll bet Samuel tore him a new one."

"Samuel doesn't accept failure well from those around him. It's possible Dax's body will turn up someplace far away from here and there will be a bullet in the back of his head."

"My recommendation to you is to lie low for the next couple days…maybe the next week. If Samuel knows you're alive, you'll be a number one priority to him and his henchmen. I'm sure he'll make his men understand that whoever brings you down will be well compensated." Hawk clapped Micah on his back. "You have now become a major liability, my friend, and you need to remove yourself."

"What about Olivia's son…Rafe's little boy? If I take myself out of this, who is going to hunt for them?"

"You know we're doing everything we can to find them," Hawk replied.

"It isn't good enough," Micah replied in frustration. "Each day that passes, the risk of those kids being whisked out of town increases and I'm afraid that once they leave Cold Plains, nobody will ever see them again." He thought of Olivia, who had been so strong through all of this.

"How's Carly?" he asked suddenly, an attempt to make Hawk think about family.

Immediately Hawk's features softened. "She's good. When this is all over and done, I'm hoping we can build a family here working her father's dairy farm."

Hawk and Carly had been romantically involved years before and then Hawk had left town and Carly had gone undercover to help save her sister who had become a cult member. In helping Carly save her sister Mia, he and Carly had rekindled their love for each other, resulting in the two of them having a small wedding with a deprogrammed Mia in attendance.

"We've just got to get this mission done," Micah said, his voice forceful with pent-up emotion. "Each moment that goes by, another person is put at risk, Samuel grows stronger instead of weaker. Somehow, some-way, we've got to figure out how to take him down."

"I know, we all know," Hawk replied. "And we're working to that end. But we're both aware of the fact that your brother has been very smart." Hawk took a step backward and turned off his flashlight. The morning sun was starting to rise, creating a faint dawn light. "The best thing you can do right now is stay out of the line of fire. Sit tight at the safe house and let us take care of things from here. Seriously, man, you're important to this mission and we can't afford to lose you."

Micah didn't reply. He had no idea why the FBI would think him so valuable to their mission. So far he felt like he'd been little help to the men who were attempting to build a case against Samuel.

"I'm serious, Micah, sit tight in the safe house and if things go bad there, the only place you'd be safe is the Pierce ranch," Hawk said.

"The Pierce ranch?" Micah looked at him in confusion. This was the first time he'd heard of the place.

"Nathan Pierce has a big spread on the outskirts of town. He lives there with his fiancée and a handful of people. It was Nathan's father, Evan, who sold Samuel Grayson the property where the creek is rumored to hold mystical healing powers, the place that ultimately became the cornerstone of Samuel's power."

"So why would I go there if things get bad?" Micah asked.

"Because none of them have bought into Samuel's teachings. The cult tried to kidnap Nathan's fiancée, Susannah, and the family fought back. They're solid in their hatred of the cult. They stay out of town as much as possible and mind their own business, but Nathan has made it clear that he can be trusted."

Micah stared at Hawk for several long moments. "You have some sort of information that the safe house location has been compromised?"

"No, nothing like that," Hawk replied quickly. "I'm just thinking that Samuel always saw you as a threat and wanted you taken out of the picture before you could hook up with the FBI. Now that he knows you're alive and here, he might push things. He might turn up the heat on finding the safe house. Let's hope if he gets frantic enough that he'll also get sloppy." Hawk shoved his hands in his pockets and reared back on his heels. "I just have a feeling that things are about to explode apart."

"They can't explode apart until we find those kids," Micah said firmly.

Hawk pulled his hands from his pocket. "Just stay put and leave that to us," he said, a hint of authority in his deep voice.

"I got it," Micah replied easily.

"Good, then I'll check in with you in the next day or so and let you know how things are going," Hawk replied. The two men said their goodbyes and Micah watched Hawk disappear the way he had come.

Micah returned to the fallen tree and once again sat, his thoughts racing. Hawk's "order" for him to stay at the safe house and out of the line of fire meant nothing to him. Micah didn't work for the FBI and he didn't take his orders from any of them.

He still didn't know why Hawk would be concerned about his safety. Sure, they had been working together as best they could, but Micah was no big piece to this puzzle. He probably knew less about his brother than the men holed up in the cabin, the agents who had probably studied every area of Samuel's life for the past five years.

Micah would lie low for a night or two, but he wasn't about to take himself out of the game. This wasn't just another job for Micah. This was a personal mission of retribution.

The moment he'd heard about Johanna's murder, he'd vowed vengeance and now it wasn't Johanna's light brown eyes that haunted him, but rather Olivia's sad green ones.

He couldn't take himself out of the game, not until he brought Ethan back to his mother's loving arms, not until he knew for sure that Samuel would never, ever hurt anyone else again.

With dawn fully breaking across the eastern sky, he headed back to the safe house, wondering what, if any, information Hawk had that he might not be sharing.

He'd said he felt as if things were about to explode apart, but, according to what Micah had heard, nothing had changed. The FBI had yet to be able to tie Samuel directly to the murdered women or any of the other dead and missing people from the small town.

They'd had almost six months to build a case. Micah had only been in the area three weeks and he already felt time slipping away too quickly.

How long would it take before the men working the case burned out, grew tired, got sloppy? How long before something bigger or more exciting drew attention and resources away from the little town of Cold Plains?

And although he knew it was crazy, he felt more than

a bit of responsibility for Samuel's sins. He'd known what Samuel was when they were young. He'd seen the cruelty, the signs of severe narcissism and sociopathic tendencies.

He should have told somebody. He should have warned someone that Samuel was capable of doing terrible things. But who would he have told? The father who beat them relentlessly? The mother who was afraid of her own shadow?

Besides, as a young kid he'd believed that if he told anyone and word got back to his father, then his father would beat Micah to death.

As he entered the safe house he carried with him the weight of both guilt and frustration. The first person he saw was Darcy, seated at the table with a cup of coffee before her.

"Good morning," he said. "You're up early."

"I woke up early and couldn't go back to sleep. I checked to see if you were in your room, but you were already gone."

He turned to look at her as he poured himself a cup of coffee. "You wanted to talk to me?" He moved to the table and sat across from her.

She looked unusually pale, her eyes filled with obvious anxiety as she nodded. "I have the picture of Jane Doe. I want to see if you recognize her." She pulled a folded piece of paper from her pocket, but seemed reluctant to push it across the table to him.

Micah knew the nervousness that had to be flooding through her. If he recognized the woman in the picture, then there was a strong possibility that it was Darcy's mother and she was dead. With a definite name, Ford

McCall could check out the background of the victim and determine for sure if she was Darcy's mother.

If he didn't recognize the woman, then she was left still wondering, still hoping for a reunion with a woman she didn't remember, but desperately needed in her life.

She finally laid the folded paper in the center of the table and he couldn't help but notice that her long, slender fingers trembled slightly.

He reached out and pulled it toward him, his heart hurting for the woman he now knew was his niece. Samuel was her father and that made it all the more important that she find out something good about her mother. She took a quick sip of her coffee as he unfolded the picture and stared down at it.

The blue eyes of the woman on the paper were definitely Darcy's eyes and Micah knew he'd seen the woman before, although it had been many years before.

He frowned, remembering who Darcy had reminded him of in the first moment of seeing her. "I remember her. She wasn't around town for long, but she was so pretty and I remember her being swept into Samuel's sphere." He looked at Darcy, hating the news he was about to deliver. "Catherine. That's definitely Catherine George."

He looked up from the picture to see tears welling up in Darcy's eyes. "She's my mother," she said as she tried to swipe at the tears that trekked down her cheeks. "He killed my mother and now I'll never have a chance to know her, to spend time with her. He stole her away from me and then he killed her."

"Maybe I'm mistaken," Micah offered, although he knew the odds of that were slim to none. "Maybe your mother is still alive and stashed someplace in Cold Plains."

Darcy shook her head and offered him a sad smile. "You don't really believe that, do you?"

Micah hesitated a moment and then shook his head. "No, but at least with her name, McCall will be able to determine if Catherine George is definitely your mother. Do you want me to contact him?"

She shook her head. "Thanks, but I'll take care of it." She rose from the table and carried her coffee cup to the sink. "I think I'm going to head back to my room and rest for a little while." With another achingly sad smile, she turned and left the kitchen.

Micah tightened his grip on his own cup, a deep ache in his chest. Jane Doe had now been identified, but would that move the investigation any farther along? He doubted it. He knew that Jane Doe's body had been found four years ago, nearly a hundred miles away from Cold Plains.

The only thing that had tied the woman to Cold Plains and Samuel was the small *D* on her right hip. It had not been tattooed on, but rather carefully drawn with a Sharpie pen. They would probably never know why she had worn a fake mark, but the odds were good she was working against the cult and Samuel and for that she had paid with her life.

And it was entirely possible that she'd given birth to Darcy and in a completely unselfish act of sacrifice had given her away so that Samuel would never know of her existence.

As he thought of Darcy's tears, a new burn started in the pit of his stomach. If the FBI thought he was just going to sit tight and hang around here for the remainder of the investigation, they were out of their mind.

He was tired of seeing Samuel's survivors and the pain that had been left behind. This had all gone on long enough and the longer it lasted the more victims there would be.

He'd lie low for tonight, but after that all bets were off. It was time he moved this game forward to some sort of conclusion, and if he didn't survive, at least he'd know he had died trying to destroy the scourge named Samuel.

Chapter 9

Olivia awakened alone in her bed, the scent of Micah lingering in the air, the warmth of him still deep in her heart. She'd slept without dreams, safe and secured by the weight of his arms around her, by the warmth of his bare legs against hers.

Micah.

Her body tingled with the sensations of their lovemaking. It had been wild and intense and had released some of the tension that had been knotted inside her since the moment she had fled Cold Plains.

But it hadn't been lovemaking, she reminded herself and she'd be a fool to think otherwise. It had been the release of sheer adrenaline, the rush of relief at being alive. It had been all kinds of things created by his wild dash for his life through the forest, but it hadn't been lovemaking.

Not hearing any noise from the nursery yet, she slid

out of the bed and threw on her clothes from the night before. She grabbed a pair of clean jeans and a T-shirt and headed for the bathroom, hoping to get in a quick shower before Sam awoke.

As she stood under the tepid, faint spray of water she tried not to think about the night before and she also tried not to think about her missing child. Both created different but very strong emotions inside her.

She finished her shower and got dressed. She spritzed her favorite perfume and thought of the man who had, in the midst of a covert operation, thought to grab the floral spray that reminded her she was a woman in this place of danger and intrigue.

By that time she heard Sam's good-morning cry coming from the nursery room. She greeted Sam with a forced happy smile as thoughts of Ethan slammed into her chest. As she changed Sam from his pajamas to his clothes for the day, her heart ached.

So many days and nights had now passed since she'd run terrified from the streets of Cold Plains. Did Ethan believe she'd abandoned him? Did he think his mommy had just given him away? Did he believe she'd forgotten all about him?

She shook her head as if to dispel the heartbreaking thoughts. She didn't want to display the piercing sadness inside her for Sam's sake. She didn't want to traumatize him anymore than she thought he already was.

With him in her arms, she mentally prepared herself not only to face another day without Ethan, but also to face Micah again.

The worst thing she could do was read too much into what had happened between them the night before, but she couldn't help that her heart had been touched by him in a way no other man had touched her. She couldn't help but wish for something more than a hot night of sex with him.

But falling in love with Micah Grayson would be just another mistake in a lifetime of bad judgment. He was a mercenary here on a job. Even though he had made a promise to her to help find Ethan, even though he'd come to her bed with fiery passion and need, that didn't mean he felt anything real and lasting for her.

He'd needed somebody last night and she'd just happened to step out of her room at the right time. She had a feeling any woman could have served the purpose he'd needed at that moment.

She was determined not to make another mistake where a man was concerned and she had a feeling loving Micah would be just that. Still, she couldn't help the way her heart jumped in her chest as she entered the kitchen and saw him seated at the table.

"Good morning," she said as she placed Sam in the high chair. "Where is everyone else?"

"Jesse and June are in the garden, Darcy went to her room a while ago and I haven't seen Lacy and her kids yet this morning. Why? Scared to be alone with me?"

She shot him a quick glance, relieved to see a teasing light in his eyes. "Not yet, but the day is still young," she replied with a light tone.

"The day might be young, but I've already met with Hawk and broken Darcy's heart."

She gave Sam a cracker to hold him over until she could make him some breakfast and looked at Micah in surprise. "What did you do to break Darcy's heart?"

She poured herself a cup of coffee and sat at the table

across from him as he told her what had transpired between him and Darcy earlier that morning.

As he told her about identifying the picture of Jane Doe and his suspicion that Catherine George was indeed Darcy's mother, Olivia's heart ached with the young woman's pain. She knew how much Darcy had hoped for some sort of happy reunion with her mother.

"She's contacting Ford to give him Catherine's name and hopefully before too long she will have a definitive answer."

"But you're sure Jane Doe is Darcy's mother."

He nodded, a weariness in his eyes. "I just feel it in my gut. I'm not sure why Catherine returned here after giving up Darcy, but I have a feeling she was either trying to save Samuel from himself or save the other people in town from Samuel."

"It's just so sad," Olivia said. She released a deep sigh. "I'm going to make some scrambled eggs and toast. You want some?" she asked.

"Are you eating?"

"Definitely. I seem to have worked up an appetite sometime during the night." She turned her back on him to grab some eggs and start breakfast, but she felt the heat of his gaze in the center of her back.

"About last night…"

She turned to face him, not wanting to hear any apologies or explanations, not wanting him to somehow take away from what had been a moment of passion in a place least expected.

"Please don't." She held up a hand to stop whatever he was about to say. "Let's not dissect, discuss or even talk about what's already done. And we don't have to get all touchy-feely about sharing emotions. Today is a new day with new challenges and we just need to get to them."

She turned back around and cracked the eggs into a bowl, hoping he took her advice. The truth of the matter was, she didn't want him to say anything that would take away the little bit of magic she'd found in his arms the night before.

Minutes later they sat at the table and laughed when Sam tried to share some of his toast with Micah, practically sticking it into his ear.

"Now that's a sound we don't hear often enough around here," June said as she and Jesse came into the kitchen. June carried a small basket of mixed vegetables and set the basket on the countertop. "That's about the last of the garden. It's getting too cold at night. If we want vegetables, we're going to have to depend on cans from now on."

"I don't want to even think about winter coming," Micah replied. "It would be nice if all of us were gone from here by the time the first snow falls."

Winter. Ethan loved wintertime. Last year during the first significant snowfall of the year, she'd bundled up the two boys in their snowsuits and they'd all gone outside to play. They'd built a snowman and she'd shown them how to make snow angels and then they'd gone back into the house with frozen fingers and toes to warm cocoa with marshmallows.

She could still remember Ethan telling her he was a snow bug as he'd rolled in a ball across the snowy yard. His laughter had accompanied each somersault and the memory caused a lump of emotion to rise up in Olivia's throat.

"What's new?" Jesse asked Micah as he poured himself a cup of coffee and joined them at the table.

As Micah told him about the flight through the forest the night before and the fact that Hawk had told him to stay out of things and let the FBI agents work the case, Olivia watched the play of emotions over Micah's face.

She could tell by the set of his jaw that he had no intention of obeying the FBI's order for him to sit tight. Even though she had no right to tell him what to do or what not to do, she wanted to tell him to listen to what the FBI had told him, to stay here, safe.

She desperately wanted her son back and she wanted Micah safe. Unfortunately, she wasn't at all sure the two were synonymous.

Most days Micah spent much of his time in his quiet little room, lying in the dark and either resting or strategizing for the night to come. But tonight he wasn't leaving the cave and there was no reason for him to isolate himself in his dark, lonely room.

Although there were plenty of people to talk to, to spend time with, he found himself drifting to wherever Olivia and Sam were located in the cave.

They were now seated in the living room area. Sam was on the floor playing with some toys that Jesse had picked up on his last trek into town for supplies.

Micah sat on the opposite end of the sofa from Olivia, but he could smell the floral scent of her perfume and liked the way her green T-shirt made her eyes appear as green as fresh spring grass.

She seemed at ease, but he knew the tumultuous emotions she had to be feeling and it frustrated him that he could do nothing about them.

"What are your plans when you leave here?" he asked, breaking the comfortable silence that had existed between them.

She tucked a strand of her pale blond hair behind her ear and looked at him. "It's hard to see a future right now. I'm just getting through minute by minute, trying not to completely freak out."

"I know." He was surprised by the small stab in his heart for her, for her pain. He'd spent most of his life trying to remain emotionless, but he couldn't succeed in that goal when it came to Olivia. "But eventually Samuel will fall, the children will be returned where they belong and life will go on. You need to be thinking about what happens when you get out of this cave."

She leaned back against the rawhide couch and frowned thoughtfully. "I love this place. The minute I saw the mountains they called to something inside me. I loved the house where we lived that had come to feel like home. Within six months of living in Cold Plains, I was certain it was going to be our home forever. The whole landscape called to something deep in my soul. I love the mountains and streams, the achingly blue skies and the wooded surroundings."

She shrugged. "But, I guess when this is over we'll move on. I have a little money saved up, enough for a two- or three-month start in a new town. I know I won't go back to Oklahoma. Maybe Colorado, where I'll have the mountains again and sparkling streams. I'll find a nice little town and start to rebuild."

"A little town where there's a local drunk and people gossip and bar fights happen on Friday nights?"

She laughed and the sound was like music. "Exactly. No more perfect towns for me. I want a place to live, blemishes and all." Her laughter died and her smile drifted off her lips. "It won't be easy. I'll be the single mother of two small boys with little training or education."

"You'll be fine. You're a strong woman, Olivia, and you're smart, smart enough to make choices that will give you a wonderful life with your sons. I see it in you and you shouldn't be afraid of whatever the future holds."

"The biggest fear I have right now is if I'm ever going to get out of this cave with both my sons," she replied drily. She snapped her mouth closed, as if she didn't want to say anything else.

He was surprised to realize that he thought he knew what she was thinking, that she desperately wanted her son back and she thought he was the man who could accomplish that, but she also didn't want him hurt or dead.

"You shouldn't worry about me," he said in a low voice.

"Why not?" Her gaze held his.

He frowned thoughtfully. "Because I'm not used to having anyone worry about me."

"Then get used to it," she countered. "Whether you like it or not, Micah, I've grown to care about you. You don't have to do anything about it. I don't expect anything in return. It's just there and that's that."

She said it all lightly, and yet the impact it had on his heart was sharp and poignant. So this was what it felt like to know that somebody cared about you? It was like a gift that he wanted to reciprocate, but he knew he shouldn't, he couldn't.

"What about you? What are your plans when this is all over?" she asked, pulling him from his thoughts.

"Are you going back to working for some covert government agency? Sneaking into foreign countries and doing mercenary kind of things?"

He started to answer flippantly, but halted himself and seriously considered her question. "To be perfectly honest, I don't know what comes after this, but I do know it's time to hang up my mercenary missions."

He leaned forward, aware that what he was about to tell her was something he'd scarcely acknowledged to himself. "The bullet in my head changed things for me. I can't trust myself anymore. I can't be truly effective anymore, never knowing if or when one of those migraines might strike."

"What have the doctors said about them?" She leaned forward as well, bringing with her the scent that had the capacity to heat the blood in his veins, make him want to carry her to his bed and claim her as his own one more time.

"They might get worse, they might get better, they could go away altogether." He shrugged. "None of the doctors are sure what will happen in the future. I've managed to put away enough funds that I can take as much time as I need to decide what comes next. Right now I just don't have any idea what that might be. Besides, I quit planning on a future when I was about eight years old and my father beat me so bad I had to miss school for a week."

He saw the jump of sympathy into her eyes and he held up a hand to halt whatever she was about to say. "I don't want your sympathy. I'm just telling you this because it made me the kind of man I am. I don't think too much about tomorrow and I don't think too much of other people."

It was a subtle warning to her not to care about him, not to give him her heart because he wouldn't have any idea what to do with it. His entire life had been about survival, nothing more, nothing less. And even when this was all over here in Cold Plains, unless they managed to round up every single one of Samuel's henchmen and fanatical Devotees, he had a feeling he'd be looking over his shoulder for a very long time to come.

They remained seated in the living room talking about everything and nothing until she got up to put Sam down for his nap.

Micah decided to head back into his own room and grab a nap, as well. The night had been too short and being around Olivia for too long of a time created a well of want inside him that he'd never felt before, that he didn't even want to acknowledge to himself.

It wasn't just desire to have her in his arms again, although that simmered inside him whenever she was near. Rather this was a wistfulness that he'd be able to listen to her laughter for a long time to come, that he'd see Sam grow up, that he'd not only save Ethan but also have the opportunity to get to know the child who had been separated from his mother for far too long.

Foolish thoughts, he told himself as he settled down on the cot in the quiet, dark room. He was born and bred to be alone and he'd only be doing Olivia a disservice if he forgot that fact for a single moment. He cared about her far too much to give her any false hope, to make her believe in any way that there was a future with him.

He fell asleep and awakened with the scent of dinner filling the air, letting him know he'd slept much longer than he'd intended.

The sound of laughter drifted from the kitchen as he

walked toward the room that was the very heart of the safe house. He could easily pick up the sound of Olivia's laughter among the others and he couldn't help the way it threatened to wrap around his heart and tie it captive. He consciously steeled himself against it, against her.

Laughter from any place in the cave was rare, but the moment he walked into the kitchen he saw the source of the merriment. Jesse was whistling an upbeat tune and Sam danced in the middle of the kitchen floor, his diapered butt beneath his little jeans shifting back and forth with each *Saturday Night Fever* move he made.

Olivia sat at the table, laughing so hard tears had sprung to her eyes and June stood at the stove, her face wreathed in a huge grin.

Jesse suddenly stopped his whistle and Sam froze in place, his gaze focused on Jesse. When Jesse began to whistle again Sam started dancing as if nothing had happened, a smile of bliss on his little face.

This caused the women to renew their laughter and Micah grinned at the small tyke who had brought even a little bit of joy to this place.

Sam toddled over to Micah and grabbed his hand, as if inviting him to join him in his dance. "Oh, no, little buddy," Micah replied and swung him up into his arms. "I'm not about to attempt dancing and let these people all laugh at me."

Sam studied him soberly and then threw his arms out, palms up as if to ask a question. "Eton?"

The laughter in the room halted abruptly and Olivia's eyes grew far too shiny with suppressed tears. Micah's heart dropped to his feet as he recognized what the little boy was asking.

"Ethan's not here right now, Sam. Ethan's gone for

now," he said, surprised at the lump that crawled up in the back of his throat as he looked into the little boy's bright eyes. "But he's going to be back very soon."

Sam stared at him for a long moment and then leaned forward and curled into him, placing his little head in the crook of Micah's neck, his breath a butterfly whisper against Micah's skin.

The sweet scent of little boy innocence, coupled with the utter trust Sam displayed as he snuggled tightly into Micah's arms, frightened Micah more than any other experience in his life.

Because he liked it. Because for just a single moment in time, he wanted this…a child who trusted him, a child who respected and loved him.

As Olivia got up and held out her arms to take her son, Micah found himself reluctant to relinquish him. Still, as he did, he made himself a new promise.

He'd abide by the wishes of Hawk and the rest of the FBI agents and lie low for tonight. He knew that Samuel's men would be pounding the pavement, turning over every rock and looking behind every tree for him in the next day or two.

But sooner or later Micah was going to ignore the advice the FBI had given him.

Sooner rather than later, he intended to head back into that town and somehow he would bring Ethan home.

Darcy raced through the dark woods, grateful that night had finally arrived. She'd spent the entire day in her room, needing to be alone, wanting the solitude to mourn the mother she knew in her heart was dead.

Twice June had come to check on her, to see if she

had wanted something to eat, if she needed some company, but each time Darcy had sent the woman away.

There was only one person Darcy wanted to see, needed to see and that was Rafe. And she'd had to wait for the cover of darkness before leaving the safe house to sneak into town.

Even though she still had to contact Ford McCall and let him do whatever he needed to do to confirm not only that Jane Doe was indeed Catherine George but also Darcy's birth mother. Even though she knew it might take a little time to confirm that the dead woman was her mother, Darcy didn't need the confirmation. She felt it in her soul that Catherine George had been the woman who had given her birth and was now dead because of Samuel Grayson.

Her father had killed her mother. How screwed up was that? As she stealthily made her way through the woods, always on the lookout for danger, she knew Rafe would be surprised to see her.

He never liked the idea of her slinking about in a town she'd supposedly left, but her need was far greater than any fear tonight.

As she reached the end of the woods, she surveyed the streets. Samuel would be in the middle of one of his nightly seminars, brainwashing his people, manipulating lives and perhaps plotting another woman's death.

She never forgot that half of her genes came from evil, but Rafe had made her realize she wasn't her father's daughter, that whatever genes of his resided inside her had nothing to do with the kind of woman she'd become.

She had no idea if Rafe would be at the 1930s converted bungalow he used as an office or if perhaps this early in the evening he'd be at the Urgent Care building where he volunteered time in an effort to network and find his missing son's location. Or he could already be home, in the small cottage at the edge of town.

It was in that direction she ran, along the perimeter of town toward the place they'd considered an asylum away from the craziness in Cold Plains.

The lights shining from the cottage were a welcomed sight as she went around to the back door and knocked. If he wasn't here, then she knew where he kept the spare key and she could let herself inside.

She knocked softly and when there was no reply she found the spare key where it was hidden behind one of the shingles and let herself inside.

The first thing she smelled when she walked through the door was the scent of Rafe's cologne, and it smelled like home. She curled up in the corner of the sofa to wait for him.

This is where she belonged, here with Rafe in this little house where they'd found such love for one another. When she'd taken the job as his receptionist, the last thing she'd had in mind was falling in love with her handsome boss, but she had and more amazing was the fact that he loved her back.

And she needed him now, with her grief a bitter taste in her mouth, with her heart broken by the shattering of the dream of a reunion with her mother.

She hadn't been there long when she heard his key in the front door. As he came into the door, his eyes widened at the sight of her. "Darcy, what are you doing here?" He quickly closed and locked the door behind him and then hurried toward her and pulled her up and into his arms.

"You shouldn't come here. You know it's dangerous," he said.

"I had to come. I needed you," she said into the front of his shirt.

He released his hold on her and instead framed her face with his palms so that she was looking at him. "What's wrong? What's happened?"

"Micah identified Jane Doe. Her name is Catherine George and I'm sure she was my mother." As the words left her lips she began to cry.

Rafe led her to the sofa and eased her down and held her until the torrent of tears had finally stopped. When the heartache was momentarily spent, she remained in his arms as he stroked the length of her hair.

"Sooner or later this will be over," he said softly. "We're going to find Devin and then we're all going to go far away from this godforsaken town. We'll find a wonderful place where we can build a life together. Devin and I will be your family and I swear you'll never feel alone again."

She clung tighter to him, hoping that his words would come true, praying that there was a happy ending not just for them but for every innocent victim of the man who was her father.

Chapter 10

Night had fallen, Sam was in bed and everyone else had disappeared into their rooms except Micah and Olivia who were once again seated on the sofa in the living room area. The room was lit with several oil lamps, creating a warm ambient glow that might feel romantic, if Micah had been a romantic kind of man.

"When I first arrived here, my only thought was getting Ethan back," Olivia said, her heartbreak shining in her eyes. "And even though that's still my first priority, now I also want Samuel gone forever and the town healed."

"We can take out Samuel, but I'm not so sure it's going to be easy to heal the town. We have no idea how deep the cancer runs in Cold Plains. Samuel isn't the only one who needs to be excised. Aside from Chief of Police Bo Fargo, who we know is crooked, there are people playing major roles in Samuel's game and we don't even know their names. They aren't even on our radar."

"What makes a town like Cold Plains?" she asked. "I mean, how does something like this happen? How does one man build such a powerful empire where so many people are simply puppets?"

It was getting late and Micah knew this was always the time of the evening when her thoughts turned to Ethan and he saw the whimpering panic beginning to simmer in her eyes. The best thing to do was to keep her talking until she grew too tired to think, too tired to grieve.

"Samuel certainly isn't the first charismatic leader to wreak havoc in people's lives. There have been lots of men before him, men like Jim Jones of the Peoples Temple and Marshall Applewhite, who got thirty-nine people to commit suicide along with him because they believed their bodies would be picked up by a passing UFO and taken to a new plane of existence beyond the human one."

"But those cults were based on religious ideas. Samuel hasn't advanced any religious ideology," she replied.

She looked so soft, so small curled into the corner of the sofa. There was nothing he wanted to do more than to reach out and pull her into his arms. Instead he focused on the conversation.

"Samuel made himself a kind of God here in town. The Community Center is his temple and his word is the law."

"But he's not even from Cold Plains. How did he gain so much power?"

Micah ran a hand through his thick dark hair and stared into the fireplace where no fire burned but logs were laid in wait for the colder months to come. The survivalist who had built the cave had vented the fireplace up through the mountain in two directions so that the smoke would be less visible if a fire burned.

"Samuel always had followers. I think before he arrived in Cold Plains he'd amassed quite a group of people who believed in him through his motivational speaking skills and charisma. Once he bought the land from old man Pierce here in town, he set about gathering those followers to this centralized location. As more new people moved in, the people who had lived here before found themselves faced with two choices, embrace the changes Samuel was making, embrace Samuel or work against him."

"And those who worked against him had unfortunate accidents, or went missing altogether," she added, her eyes dark.

He nodded. "I'm sure some of the townspeople were thrilled that somebody had come in and was making updates, cleaning everything up and taking them from a rough-and-rowdy town into something nicer and more upscale. Unfortunately, they didn't realize the price they paid was their soul to the devil."

He frowned thoughtfully, thinking of the way his brother had accomplished his goals. "There's definitely a group mentality at play. Samuel is good at fostering the 'you're with us or against us' kind of mentality. He creates an 'in' crowd and it's uncool not to belong. Peer pressure isn't just felt by teenagers and can be a terrible thing when it comes to situations like this."

She was silent for a long moment, her gaze troubled as she stared at the fireplace and then looked at him once again. "I've never heard any rumors about Samuel actually hurting children."

"I've never heard anything like that, either," he assured her, realizing that their discussion hadn't taken her mind off her missing son at all. "Samuel sees children like commodities to be sold. In Devin's case, he knew that Abby Michaels was dead so Devin became a candidate for an illegal adoption. With you missing and no father in the picture, that makes Ethan an adoptable commodity, as well. The absolute worst thing that could happen to Ethan and Devin is that they'll be sold out for adoption." She winced at his words. "But, the FBI have been checking vehicles leaving town and they feel certain the children are still there."

"But nobody knows where," she replied flatly. She rubbed a hand across her forehead, as if attempting to numb a headache. "Maybe I should go back to town. I could leave Sam here and make up some story about the FBI questioning me or something. I could tell everyone that I knew Wilma Lathrop would take care of Ethan in my absence." She dropped her hand back to her lap.

"Who is Wilma Lathrop?" he asked. It was a name he hadn't heard before.

"She's an older woman who works at the day care. She's sweet and very good with the kids. I'm hoping that she's taking care of Ethan in my absence."

"I'll tell you right now, you aren't going back into town," Micah said forcefully.

"But it might be the only way I can get information about where Ethan is being held," she protested.

"So, you're just going to waltz up to Samuel or one of his minions and ask where Ethan is after what you saw him do, not knowing if he saw you witness his crime that night? Olivia, if I have to hog-tie you to your bed, you aren't going back into that town."

"You wouldn't hog-tie me to the bed," she scoffed.

"Don't test me, Olivia," he warned.

She released a deep sigh. "If anyone needs to be tied up to keep them from going to town, it's you."

"I have no intention of going into town tonight."

She eyed him dubiously. "And what about tomorrow night or the night after that? The FBI have basically told you to stand down and stay out of sight. Are you going to listen to them?"

"I'm here, aren't I?" He didn't want her to know that he had every intention of returning to town. He'd made her a promise and even though she'd attempted to release him from it, he wouldn't be satisfied until she had her son back.

"You scare me, Micah."

He looked at her in surprise. "Scare you? Why?"

"I'm not scared of you hurting me or anything like that, but I'm afraid of you doing something to hurt yourself, taking chances you shouldn't take. I know I've been a neurotic crybaby where Ethan is concerned, but I don't want you to sacrifice yourself for him."

"You haven't been a crybaby. On the contrary, I think you've been amazingly strong through this whole thing," he replied. This time he couldn't fight the impulse that he'd been combating since the instant they had both sat down.

He leaned forward and touched her arm and she came willingly forward as if she'd just been waiting for the right moment. She leaned into him, her head resting on his chest, her body warm and softly feminine against his.

"I'm not sure how I could have handled all this without you here," she said.

He stroked the softness of her hair, the scent of her filling his nose, half-dizzying his brain. "You would have been fine without me here. You're going to be just fine when this is all over."

She was quiet for several minutes and then broke the silence. "Do you ever think about getting married... having a family?" She didn't raise her head to look at him.

About a million times since the moment he'd met her, he'd thought about what it would be like to come home to the same woman every night, to have a family to care for, to laugh with and to share a future with people he loved...with people who loved him. And each time he had imagined it, it was her he came home to and Sam and Ethan that greeted him at the door, that filled his life. But he didn't say this out loud.

"Never," he lied. "I don't want the burden. I've always traveled alone. That's what I'm used to, that's the way I like it." Funny that his words were in such a direct contrast to the fact that she was cuddled in his arms and he didn't want to let her go.

"That's too bad," she replied softly. "I have a feeling you would have made some lucky woman a wonderful husband, and seeing you with Sam makes me believe you would be a terrific father."

"I wouldn't have the first idea on how to be a father, given the role model I had," he replied.

"Being a parent is easy. All you have to do is love and allow yourself to receive love."

She raised her head to look at him, her green eyes warm and inviting. "And you are worthy of being loved,

Micah." It was at that moment he knew that if he allowed himself to, he could love this woman.

However he wouldn't allow it. Even though he'd decided that this would be his last mission, if he looked deep in his heart, deep in his very soul, he'd admit that he wasn't at all sure he was going to survive this, his final mission.

"There was definitely a chill in the air today," June said as she, Olivia and Darcy sat at the kitchen table eating dinner. Sam sat in his high chair, happily enjoying some of June's homemade applesauce and macaroni and cheese.

"Where are Lacy and her daughters?" Darcy asked.

"They were relocated last night," June replied. A touch of sadness darkened her eyes. "I'm going to miss those two little girls. They were such delights."

"It must be hard doing what you do," Olivia said. "Building relationships with people and then moving on to the next cult, the next victims." Her thoughts immediately went to Micah, who hadn't been seen all day. She tried telling herself that the building love she had for him was based on nothing more than the situation. Their enforced closeness had sent hormones into high drive, but she knew when this was all over she'd probably never see him again.

"That is the most difficult part of what I do," June replied. "It's hard not to build relationships in situations like this. But this is Eager's and my last job for a while." The black Lab lying on the floor nearby raised his head and looked at her.

"Doggie," Sam exclaimed and smiled at Olivia.

"That's right, doggie," Olivia agreed.

"You're going with Jesse to his ranch," Darcy said.

A smile swept over June's features, a smile of such love, of such happiness that it ached a little bit in Olivia's chest. "He says Eager will be kept busy chasing rabbits and I'm going to be busy chasing him."

They all laughed but Olivia felt a wistful envy raise its head inside her. Someday she wanted what June had found, the love of a good man who would be willing to step in and parent her sons, a man who would love her desperately, passionately until the end of time.

Each and every time she thought of such a man it was Micah who jumped into her head, but she knew that was just a ridiculous fantasy she had to get over.

Last night as they'd snuggled together on the sofa, he'd made it clear to her that he didn't want to be part of a family, that he wasn't a man looking for love or commitment.

But at the moment, with Ethan still a crushing pain in her heart and the uncertainty of ever seeing him again, the last thing on her mind was love. She just wanted her baby boy back and then she'd figure the rest of her life out from there.

She turned her attention to Darcy, who had been unusually quiet throughout the day. "Are you doing okay?" she asked.

Darcy nodded. "I saw Rafe last night and we called Ford McCall and told him that Micah had identified Jane Doe. He's going to do what he can to confirm that she's the woman who gave birth to me."

"Ford's a good man," June replied.

"It's amazing he's been able to work with that skunk, Chief of Police Fargo," Darcy said.

"Bo Fargo isn't just a skunk," June said with narrowed

eyes. "He's a dangerous man who has been given far too much power by Samuel. I wouldn't be surprised if he was the one who actually put the bullets in those poor women. Jesse believes that the good police chief is one of the men who beat him half to death and left him for dead in the woods."

For a moment they all fell silent. Olivia had no idea what the others were thinking but she was thinking about men like Bo Fargo holding her child captive someplace. She fought against the tears that burned behind her eyelids, refusing to allow them to fall here in the presence of her youngest son and the other women.

Jesse came in from the outside where he had been standing guard, indicating that somebody else had taken over for him. He wore a thick plaid jacket and brought with him the scent of the cold, fresh outdoor air.

"There's a thick layer of fog moving in," he said as he took off his jacket and slung it over the back of an empty chair at the table. "I have a feeling in another hour or so you won't be able to see your hand in front of your face."

"A good night for all God's children to stay inside and be safe," June said.

"Or a good night to create some mischief," Micah said as he came into the kitchen. He smiled at Olivia and she consciously willed her heart not to quicken.

"I hope you don't intend to make any mischief," she said.

"Not me, but I want to talk to Hawk and make sure that they're setting up traffic stops coming in and out of town," he replied as he sat across from her at the table.

He didn't have to say why he wanted to check on that. Olivia knew what he was thinking, that the cover of fog might provide a perfect opportunity to move two unwanted, highly adoptable children out of the area. If the FBI agents in the area weren't careful, tonight was the night she could potentially lose her child forever.

Once again the group fell silent as June busied herself fixing plates for both Jesse and Micah. After they'd been served, the conversation remained light and neutral, but Olivia's heart thundered with the idea of Ethan vanishing for good.

As she exchanged glances with Darcy, she knew the young woman shared the same concern about Rafe's son. Micah looked at her, his eyes slightly hard and filled with resolve. "We're not going to let those kids get away from us," he said, obviously reading her mind.

She nodded. Although she knew rationally it was impossible for a single man to control what was happening in and around an entire town, in her heart she desperately wanted to believe him.

After eating, as the women cleared the table, Micah left the safe house, she assumed for his meeting with Hawk or one of the other FBI agents working the case.

She knew she wouldn't breathe easily again until he returned. She lifted Sam from the high chair and carried him into the living room, followed by Darcy.

With Sam on one of the thick hide rugs with a pile of toys in front of him, the two women sat on the sofa. "I'm sorry about your mother," Olivia said.

Darcy gave her a bittersweet smile. "I think maybe I've always known deep in my heart that it wasn't going to be a happy ending for me, but I'd hoped..." She allowed her voice to trail off as her gaze lingered on Sam. "At least I have Rafe and hopefully before too long we'll have Devin and you'll have Ethan back."

"We can only hope," Olivia replied.

"You're in love with Micah, aren't you?"

Olivia looked at Darcy in shock and then was unable to control the nervous little laugh that escaped her. "Why on earth would you think such a thing?"

Darcy shot her a smug little smile. "Because you look at him the way I know I look at Rafe. Because I see the worry in your eyes each time he leaves this place."

"I worry about everyone when they leave here," Olivia countered.

Darcy smiled knowingly. "But you worry just a little bit more about Micah."

Olivia released a small sigh. "It doesn't matter what I feel toward him. This is just a crazy stop on our way to the rest of our separate lives. I mean, look around… We are sitting in a cave because a madman has taken possession of an entire town. Could it get more surreal?"

"It just goes to show that love can blossom in the strangest of places," Darcy replied.

"Trust me, Micah has made it very clear that love has no place in his life." A piercing sadness swept through Olivia for the man who had never known love as a child, for the man who had chosen to live his life alone. "Micah told me that you're his niece. I only hope that he'll allow you and Rafe and Devin to be the family he never had."

"I'd like that," Darcy agreed. She eyed Olivia soberly. "It doesn't bother you to know that Samuel is my biological father?"

Olivia smiled. "Darcy, I have no idea who my father is and my mother was a raging alcoholic who only got out of bed to get another bottle of booze. Unfortunately, we don't get to pick our parents. You are nothing like your father and in a million years nothing could make you like him."

Darcy reached over and grabbed Olivia's hand in hers. "I hope you find happiness when you leave here, Olivia. I hope you find a good man to love you and your two boys. We all deserve happiness after what we've been through."

"I definitely agree with that," Olivia replied.

At that moment Micah returned, his restless energy filling the entire living room. "Hawk has promised me that nothing is going to leave town tonight that we don't know about," he said. "The fog, along with the narrow roads that lead in and out of town, should make travel for anyone slow, and that works to our advantage."

He was amped up, much like he had been the night he'd come home after nearly being caught in the forest and had taken her to bed. The pump of adrenaline rolled off him in waves and his eyes had taken on the glittering of an animal on the prowl.

She knew in that moment that despite what he'd been told by the FBI to sit tight, that he was going out to do something dangerous, that he intended to use the fog cover for his own purposes.

"What are your plans?" she asked, unable to control the slight tremor in her voice.

"I'll just leave you two to talk," Darcy said as she jumped up from the sofa and hurried from the room, leaving Olivia and Micah alone.

"Nothing for you to worry about," he said as he started out of the room.

She followed behind him. "What does that mean?"

They passed the bedrooms and she stared at his back,

willing him to halt, to turn around and tell her he intended to spend the rest of the night in the safe house.

He didn't reply until they reached the tiny room where he slept. An oil lamp was lit, the illumination bouncing off the rocky walls. There was a single-sized cot and several canvas bags lined up against one wall.

He leaned over and picked up one of the canvas bags, then turned to face her. "With the fog it's a perfect night to check out a few places in town."

Olivia's heart pounded with anxiety as she stared at him with a horrible sense of dread. "I don't want you to go."

She took a step toward him, wondering if he could hear the thunder of her heart in the small space. "Stay here with me, Micah. You know it's too dangerous for you to go out there tonight."

He placed a warm palm against her cheek, his eyes holding both a softness and a distance that let her know he was already half-gone from her. "This is what I do, Olivia."

He dropped his hand from her face and left the room with her trailing behind him, trying to think of something, anything that would keep him here with her. He'd been told to stay out of things, to stay away from town. Why oh why wasn't he listening to the FBI...to her?

They reached the entrance to the cave and he turned to face her, his eyes already holding the wildness of the forest, of whatever mission he had in mind for the night.

He paused and dropped the duffel bag he carried to the floor and then wrapped her in his arms and pressed his mouth to hers in an intense kiss that tasted far too much like goodbye.

She clung to him, fighting tears as the kiss lingered.

He was breaking her heart. By leaving here, by kissing her the way he was, he was truly shattering her apart.

He finally released her and once again grabbed the duffel bag. With a curt nod of his head, he stepped out of the opening of the safe house and she desperately feared that she would never see him again.

Chapter 11

The fog had created a false sense of twilight as Micah stepped out into the woods. Although not as thick here as it would be in the lower valley that held the town of Cold Plains, the fog could definitely work for him or against him.

It would be more difficult for anyone to spot him, but it would also make it harder for him to see danger coming. Still, he felt no fear as he made his way down the mountain toward town.

In the distance a wolf howled, the sound mournful as it resonated deep in Micah's soul. Micah had always considered himself a lone wolf, but that was a mischaracterization of the wild animal. Even wolves lived in packs, with a mate and their offspring.

He shoved these thoughts away as he continued down the mountain. The farther down he went, the thicker the fog grew, enveloping him in a gray mist that stirred a faint anxiety inside him.

With each step he took, he stopped and listened, making sure there wasn't anyone else near him in the soupy fog. The dense mist seemed to amplify even the tiniest natural sound, making him more jumpy than usual.

One hand gripped the handle of the duffel bag and the other held tight to his gun. He finally reached the edge of Cold Plains and crouched behind a large tree trunk.

From this vantage point the only thing visible in the town was the barely discernible muted glow from the streetlamps. Micah set down the duffel bag and checked his watch. Five minutes until seven.

He'd sit tight for now and wait for the ring of the old church bell that would summon all the townspeople to Samuel's nightly seminar. Only when he knew his brother was busy shepherding his sheep would Micah make his bold move.

He'd spent most of yesterday working things around in his head, trying to think how his brother would when it came to safety and secrets.

He knew about the tunnel that ran underground beneath the Community Center. He also knew that hidden rooms had been found below the Urgent Care facility. But he couldn't imagine a man as crafty as Samuel sleeping in bed at night in a house that had no escape route but the front and back doors. It just didn't make "Samuel sense."

It was imperative that Micah got inside Samuel's house tonight and found out what secrets might be contained within its impressive walls. And this was the perfect night. While Samuel was leading his flock, Micah intended to check it out.

At precisely eight o'clock the church bell tolled, the sound muted and discordant as it traveled through the dense fog. Micah waited another ten minutes and then left the safety of his hiding place.

As usual he stuck to the backyards and what cover he could find, but the fog made it slow going as he could only see approximately a foot in front of him.

It took him much longer than he'd anticipated to finally reach the back of Samuel's house. Using the cover of the trees, he pulled the grappling hook and rope from the duffel bag and then watched to see if the guard presence had increased since the last time he'd been here.

Samuel's seminars generally lasted between an hour and an hour and a half. Micah couldn't wait too long to make his move or he wouldn't have the time he needed to explore the interior of the house.

He heard rather than saw somebody moving around the back of the house. As he watched with narrowed eyes, trying to pierce through the veil of fog, the man stopped and flicked a lighter to light a cigarette. The resulting glow from the lighter illuminated his features for just a moment and Micah identified him as the second guard who had chased him through the forest with Dax Roberts.

The man moved on and when Micah could no longer hear the whisper of his feet against the grass, he made his move. Although he couldn't see the balcony ledge above him, he made a calculated throw of the hook and fought against the triumphant cry he wanted to release as the hook didn't return to the ground.

Going up would be easy. Micah had climbed ropes a thousand times in his lifetime. Coming down could be more difficult because, in order to leave no trace of his presence, he'd have to remove the grappling hook and jump with it and the rope in his arms.

He raced to the rope and tugged on it to make sure it was secure and then like a spider climbed. Once he was secure on the balcony, he pulled up the rope behind him and unfastened the hook from where it had grabbed on the wooden railing.

He left the hook and rope on the balcony and turned to the glass sliding doors. Holding his breath, he reached out and slid the door open.

Bingo. He knew Samuel would be arrogant enough to believe that the security he had in place was enough. Samuel would have never believed anyone would have the courage to breach his privacy even with an unlocked door.

The first thing Micah looked for was any indication that there was a security system in place, but he saw no panel blinking a warning, nothing that would make him believe that, electronically, somebody knew he was inside.

A shine of his flashlight let him know he was in the master bedroom. The room was palatial, the furnishings fit for a king. Micah's heart thundered a million beats a minute as he checked his watch. Too much time had passed, the fog had slowed him down. To be safe, he could only allow himself fifteen, twenty minutes tops, inside.

If there was any place in the house where there might be a secret escape route, Micah thought it would be here in the bedroom. There was no way Samuel would allow himself to be caught sleeping by an FBI raid or any other enemies that might make it into the house.

A stone fireplace took up the center of the wall opposite the bed. Above the mantel a huge television hung, and on either side of that, fine paintings surely bought and paid for by illegal means.

One entire wall was bookcases filled with not only tomes on self-motivation and achieving success, but also containing lovely vases and ornate sculptures arrayed in artful design. Samuel definitely enjoyed the finer things in life.

The other wall held an easy chair, a small table and a reading lamp. In front of the chair was an oversized oval Oriental rug in vibrant colors.

Micah had seen enough old movies to know that the best guess for some sort of secret passageway was behind one of the bookshelves. Would Samuel be so predictable?

Aware of the seconds quickly ticking off, Micah moved to the mahogany wooden cases and used his penlight to see if he could find some sort of mechanism that would move them in any way.

He realized at some point his main mission had changed. He still wanted to bring down Samuel, but more than that he wanted to return the missing Ethan to Olivia's arms. There would be others that would continue to work on getting Samuel to justice. He wasn't sure when, but at some point avenging Johanna's death had become second to healing Olivia's heart.

After a few minutes of searching, far too conscious of time constraints, he moved to the fireplace. There was no sign that a fire had ever burned in the ornate stone hearth and he climbed up into it, seeking a false back or something that would yield to a secret saferoom or passage.

Nothing. He checked his watch again and thought

about looking in other rooms, but the residence was massive and he was convinced that if there was an escape route anyplace in the house it would be here, in Samuel's bedroom.

He stood in the center of the room, seeking something, anything that might give him a clue. Something that didn't quite fit. Something that wasn't quite right with the room. Was he wrong? Was it possible that the rat didn't have a getaway hole from this space? Maybe there was an escape route in the bathroom, in the hallway. Hell, it could be anywhere in the house. He'd just thought the bedroom made the most sense.

He knew the odds of him having the opportunity to get back into this house again were minimal and he'd so wanted to go back to Olivia with some kind of news. Dammit, he'd wanted to be her hero.

Checking his watch once again, he flashed his penlight one last time around the room, the beam stopping on the Oriental rug. It felt just a little too big for the space. The settlers had used rugs to cover the entrance to root cellars where they could hide from marauding Indians. Was it possible?

He raced over to the rug and lifted it, his heart jumping in stunned surprise as beneath it he found a wooden door. *Score,* he thought as he pulled open the door and shone his light down a dark, narrow staircase.

Drawing a deep breath, praying that he had time enough to check it out and then get the hell out of here before his presence was discovered, he started down the stairs.

It felt as if he was heading into the very bowels of the earth before the staircase finally ended and he stepped into a narrow corridor lit by several dim light bulbs hanging from the ceiling.

Just ahead he saw a single doorway on the left side of the corridor that appeared to go on forever beyond the door. *You're running out of time,* an inner voice screamed in his head. He ignored it, moving closer to the closed door.

He froze as he heard a childish cry come from behind the door. The children. This had to be where Samuel was keeping Devin and Ethan.

"I want my mommy," the child cried. "I want my brother. I want Sammy."

His heart crashed in his chest, torn between the need to rush in and rescue and the intelligence to know that he'd never get out of this house alive with both children in tow.

As much as he didn't want to leave, he knew the smartest thing he could do right now was save himself so he could make plans with Hawk and the other men for an all-out assault that would assure the children's safety. As much as he wanted to, he couldn't act alone tonight.

He backed away, turned and raced up the stairs. Once he was again in the bedroom, he carefully closed the door and rearranged the rug the way it had been over the opening.

He wasn't home free yet. He still had to get out of the house and he knew that time was running out. Samuel rarely dawdled once his seminars were over and that bell calling the meeting to start had rung just over an hour ago.

Out on the balcony, he grabbed his hook and rope and then tried to peer down below. The fog was still so thick he couldn't see the ground. He had no idea where the guards might be or how soon one of them might round the side of the house.

If he jumped and landed wrong, he could break a leg or severely injure himself. That would put him in the hands of the guards, and he knew there would definitely be no mercy for him.

He crawled over the balcony edge and listened for the sound of anyone approaching. He heard nothing and he grabbed the lower part of the balcony railing, hung his body down as low as he could and then dropped.

The hard ground met him sooner than he'd expected, but he hit the earth with his knees bent and went straight into a roll to absorb some of the impact.

With his heart still crashing a mad rhythm, he darted in the direction of his duffel bag and then had to click on his flashlight to find it. He shoved the hook and rope inside the bag and then paused to draw several long, slow breaths.

Samuel's meeting would be breaking up by now, but Micah wasn't ready to return to the safe house yet. He'd found the entrance to the secret corridor inside the house but he didn't intend to go home until he'd found the exit and he knew that would probably be someplace in the wooded area behind the house.

Finding it was going to be a challenge, not only because Samuel was crafty, but also because of the fog that shrouded everything.

The good news was that he thought the exit was far enough away from the house that he wasn't too worried about encountering the guards. If he couldn't see them, then they couldn't see him, either.

He worked in a grid search fashion, methodically

checking every rock, every bush, every odd formation that the landscape had to offer.

He didn't expect to find anyone on guard at the exit point. Samuel wouldn't want to draw that kind of attention to it. If he was to guess, nobody, including Samuel's top men, knew about this particular escape route. He would have kept the information all to himself. Probably the only other person who did know about it was whoever was in charge of taking care of the children.

He found it just before dawn, hidden by a thick prickly bush that when pushed slightly aside revealed an earthen staircase going underground. He mentally marked the area using natural landmarks and then, realizing the sun was rising and slowly burning off the fog, he headed back to the safe house.

Happiness soared through him, a happiness he'd never known before. If all went right then by this time tomorrow Olivia would be reunited with her son. Her heart would be full and he couldn't wait to see the unadulterated joy light her beautiful eyes. He couldn't wait for the moment her family was whole once again.

Of course, his happiness was tempered by the fact that once she had Ethan back, it would be time for her to be relocated. The thought of not seeing her every day broke something inside him he hadn't been aware existed.

He loved her, but he had to let her go. She had a life to live far away from this town and Samuel Grayson. It was right that she move on. She deserved a man who knew more than Micah would ever know or be able to learn about love. She'd find some small town and a good man to love her and her children. He had to believe that.

It was the only way this would work. Once the kids

were back where they belonged, Micah still had work to do. He had to make sure his brother didn't manage to somehow weasel his way out of an arrest or escape altogether.

It had been an endless night and by the time dawn broke, Olivia fought against a hysteria she'd only felt once before. The night she'd run after seeing Samuel kill that man. The night she'd had to leave one of her precious sons behind.

Micah. Her heart had cried with each agonizing minute that passed, every hour that crept by. Where was he? Had he been taken captive by one of Samuel's men? Was he dead? Surely she would know if he'd been killed. Surely she would have felt his death at her very core.

When he walked through the door just after dawn, she threw herself into his arms, weeping at the very sight of him unharmed.

"Hey, hey," he exclaimed as he dropped the duffel bag to the floor and grabbed her to him. "What's all this?"

"I was afraid you were gone forever, that somebody had either caught you or killed you," she sobbed into the front of his jacket.

"Do you really think I'd let any of those bozos in town catch or kill me?" he replied lightly.

"Those bozos are dangerous." Her voice was half-muffled by both his jacket and her choked sobs.

"Come on, we don't want to wake up anyone else," he said. He led her to her room, where he pulled her inside and closed the door.

She burrowed into his chest and leaned into his body

seeking to warm the icy chill that had overtaken her as she'd awaited his return.

She looked up at him, tears still streaking down her cheeks. "I've been so afraid for you."

He used his thumbs to swipe away her tears. "Nobody has ever cried for me before," he said softly. "Besides, now isn't the time for crying. I think I found where the children are being held."

Her eyes widened as she stared up at him. "What... where? Oh, Micah, we need to go get them." She spun out of his arms and grabbed his hand, a warrior mother ready to go claim her missing child.

"Whoa, we can't do anything right now. It would be far too dangerous." He led her to the bed and pulled her down next to him and explained what he had done and what he'd discovered since he'd been gone.

Any weariness she might have felt from the night of worry dissipated as she listened to what he had found and the fact that he'd heard a child cry, a child who had cried for her and for his little brother. Had it been Ethan? Had her baby been crying for her? A piercing ache shot through her heart and she began to cry again, unable to control the emotions that tumbled inside her.

"Shhh." Micah pulled her back into his arms. "It's going to be okay, Olivia. I'll meet with Hawk sometime later this morning and make arrangements to get those kids out of there later tonight when Samuel is holding his evening meeting. You just need to stay strong for a little while longer."

"I can do that," she said, reluctant to move from the warmth and strength of his arms. But she knew what he needed more than anything at the moment. Sleep. If he was planning on some sort of attack in town tonight to retrieve her son, then he needed to rest. He'd been up all night long and so had she, worrying about him. She hoped to get an hour or two of rest before Sam awakened and the day officially began.

"Olivia, this will probably be our last time together," he said and she could feel the quickening of her heart against her own. "Once Ethan is back here, I'll make arrangements for you and your children to be immediately taken from this area. We'll see to it that you're relocated someplace where you can begin to build a new life."

She leaned back and looked at him, loving him with all her heart. "What about you? You know I'm in love with you."

His eyes darkened and he looked away from her. "I'm sorry that's happened." He drew a deep breath and then looked at her once again. "Olivia, you've made me feel things I've never felt before. You've been the sun in this godforsaken cave." His voice grew thick with emotion. "But I'm just another bad choice for you. I have a job to finish here and there's no room in my life for you and the boys."

She searched his features, wanting something different from him. She saw love for her in the depths of his eyes, felt it in his every touch. She was certain that he loved her, and yet she was absolutely powerless to stop him from turning his back on what could be.

The last thing she intended to do was beg for his love, for some sort of a commitment that when this nightmare was over they would find a way to be together.

He'd made her a promise that he would find her son and return him to her. Once that promise was done, he intended to walk away from her without a backward glance.

Knowing that these were the last moments they would ever have alone, she leaned up and pressed her lips against his, wanting to taste him, to feel him one remaining time.

"Then I want to make one final bad choice," she said. "Make love to me, Micah. Give me memories to carry with me when I leave here."

His eyes flared hot at her words. "That would be a sweet memory I would carry with me, too," he replied.

There was little talk after that. Within minutes they were both naked and in her bed and Olivia's mind emptied of everything but Micah. She drew in the scent of him, memorized the feel of his skin against hers, the sensations his every touch crashed through her.

This time the wildness was gone, replaced by a slow, sweet tenderness that was every bit as exciting as the first time they'd had sex.

This time she was truly making love to him and whether he admitted it or not, he was making love to her, as well. Their bodies moved together as if they'd been partners forever, as if they were made to fit together perfectly.

Joined together, his hands caressed down her back as his lips nibbled gently on her neck. He breathed her name and in the three syllables of the single word she felt more loved than ever before.

As he moved his body back and forth against hers, she placed her hands on the sides of his hips, loving the feel of his warm skin beneath her hands.

When he deepened his thrusts, pleasure swept through her, building to a point where every nerve in her body sang. As the sensations reached a crescendo, she held tight to him and cried out his name as she rode the waves of her orgasm. With a deep guttural moan, he stiffened against her as he found his own release.

When it was over, a bittersweet pain and pleasure filled her as she fell asleep, knowing that she would never experience the wonder of loving Micah again.

She awoke some time later, alone in the bed and feeling fully rested. A glance at her watch told her it was just after noon. She jumped out of bed, aware that somebody had been caring for Sam as she slept.

While the people here worked together as a family, helping each other out, she didn't like to burden anyone with the caretaking of her son. Still, she'd slept hard and now all her heart felt was the sweet anticipation of finally getting Ethan back.

She consciously didn't think about final goodbyes to Micah. She found everyone in the kitchen gathered around the table. Sam sat in his high chair and greeted her with a happy smile. She returned his smile absently and ruffled the fine hair on his head, her gaze focused on the three men seated at the table she didn't know.

"Olivia." Micah stood and gestured her toward an empty chair next to him. As she sat down, she noticed that he looked rested and alert and this was obviously a planning meeting for getting the children out of Cold Plains.

He gestured to a sandy-haired man. "This is Special Agent Hawk Bledsoe. He's going to be coordinating our movements this evening with the FBI. The two men with him are Agents Randy Avery and Lyle Kincaid. Both men have been working undercover in town."

"We've already determined that the best time to go

in for the children is during Samuel's nightly meeting. Most of the town will be at the Community Center and out of our way," Randy said.

"I'll go in through the exit hole I found and grab whatever kids are in that room down the corridor. You all wait and guard the entrance. If we're quiet, then not even the guards on Samuel's house will have any idea that something is happening. Once those kids are free, the most important thing is to get them out of town and back here to the safe house. After that's done, all bets are off for whatever you want to do as far as arresting Samuel and any of his minions."

"Oh, there're going to be arrests tonight," Hawk said, his eyes narrowing. "We're going to tear this town apart tonight and when we're finished, hopefully there won't be a bad guy left standing without wearing a pair of handcuffs."

"Finding those kids beneath Samuel's house was the break we've been waiting for," Lyle exclaimed. "We can get Samuel arrested for unlawful imprisonment, kidnapping and any number of other charges and once we have him, I have a feeling there's going to be a lot of singing going on from the others."

"Everyone arrested is going to want to make a deal to save themselves and that means they'll be pointing fingers at their leader and hopefully, when all is said and done, we'll have enough evidence to put Samuel away for the rest of his life," Randy replied.

They made it sound so easy, Olivia thought. Get in, grab the children, get out and make arrests. But nobody had mentioned that Samuel's men wouldn't go down without a fight, that Samuel himself would shoot to kill anyone he thought might be a threat.

The night was fraught with danger, their plan definitely not infallible. Olivia's heart banged hard against her chest as she realized some of the people sitting at this very table might not survive the mission.

Chapter 12

The plans were made. When the church bell tolled the hour of eight, the action would begin. At seven-fifteen Micah left his room in the cave and headed for the exit. His progress was halted by Olivia, who was clad in black pants, a long-sleeved black shirt and even had her shiny blond hair tucked into a black stocking cap.

"What are you doing?" he asked. "Playing ninja?"

She flashed him a look of annoyance. "I'm not playing at anything. I'm going with you." She raised her chin as if prepared to battle whatever protest he might throw her way.

He didn't disappoint her. "The hell you are. You're going to stay right here out of the range of danger." He motioned for her to step aside so he could continue, but she held her ground before him.

"I can either go with you or without you, but nobody, not even you, is keeping me here while you go after my son. You need me, Micah," she said desperately. "These are children and they'll be frightened by the sight of you storming in the room dressed all in black and grabbing them up. Besides, how can you use your gun if necessary if you have Devin in one arm and Ethan in the other?" She flushed, as if she were aware that she was talking too much, too fast, but he also saw the fierce determination shining from her eyes.

She reached out and placed her small hand in the center of his chest. "Please, Micah. I'm the one who left him behind and if I don't participate in trying to get him back, I'll go absolutely insane."

"What about Sam?" Surely she wouldn't want to leave Sam here without her.

"Darcy has agreed to stay here and watch him. She's good with him so I know he'll be fine." She pulled her hand away from him, but continued to hold his gaze intently.

Although the last thing he wanted to do was place her in any danger, part of what she said made sense. The plan required Micah to get into the tunnel, get the kids and then get out of there with as little noise as possible. If Ethan screamed and cried as he dragged him from the room, then it was possible all hell would break loose. And the last thing he wanted was any chaos in or around town until those kids were out safe and sound.

"Okay," he finally said. "You can come with me on one condition. You listen to every order I give you and you instantly obey. I don't want you putting yourself or anyone else in danger."

She nodded. "I can follow rules."

He hesitated another moment, but he could see in

her eyes that she hadn't been bluffing. With or without him, she intended to leave the safe house tonight.

"Okay, come on. We've got to get moving now." He turned and headed for the exit, hoping this all wasn't a mistake. As they stepped out into the night air, Micah was grateful that it was a night with thick clouds across the sky, obscuring not only the millions of stars that were normally visible, but also any sight of the nearly full moon.

As he began his trek down the mountain, he was pleased that Olivia moved quickly and lightly, making little noise as she followed directly behind him.

His muscles had tensed the moment they'd left the safe house, prepared for success…and afraid of failure. This was it. He knew they'd only get one chance at this and if they didn't get it done right, then the kids would disappear from Cold Plains forever.

He knew Olivia must feel the same way…the tensed muscles, the frantic beat of her heart, the knowledge that failure was a distinct possibility.

The plan was for Micah to get the kids to safety and then the FBI intended to move in and make arrests. There would be bedlam in the perfect little town tonight and it would take months for the FBI to clean up the mess, figure out who to charge with what and who to release or hold on charges.

Of course by that time, his hope was that Olivia and her two boys would be relocated someplace where they would be safe and happy and Micah…? He hadn't quite figured out what his next move would be. Once Samuel was behind bars, Micah would have time to figure out what he intended to do for the rest of his life.

He couldn't think about that now. He had to stay

focused on the next thirty to forty-five minutes when everything was at stake for the investigation…and for Olivia. This was the most important mission he would ever attempt and never had he wanted success as much as now.

Neither of them spoke as they continued through the forest. Micah knew that in all areas of the town, men were getting into position, awaiting word from him that the children had been saved and they could move in.

The closer they got to the exit of the tunnel that Micah had found, the harder his heart banged inside his chest. Olivia remained just behind him, stepping where he stepped, mirroring his movements in an effort to be completely silent.

Micah had given Hawk the coordinates to the exit and the FBI man was to meet Micah there, along with a couple other men.

For backup.

For unexpected trouble.

He stopped suddenly, Olivia bumping into his back as he caught the sound of something moving to the left of them. Whatever it was sounded big and didn't seem to attempt to hide the noise it was making.

With his finger firmly on his gun trigger, he flipped on his flashlight and caught sight of a moose in the distance. A small gasp escaped Olivia at the view of the magnificent creature. The animal shied away from the light and Micah and Olivia moved on.

That's what should be in these mountainous woods, elk and deer, moose and bear, not killers and survivors of the human kind, Micah thought.

They finally reached the bush behind which the tunnel existed, but nobody else was there yet. He pointed

Olivia toward a thick tree trunk and together they stepped behind it to hide and wait for Hawk and his men.

He wrapped an arm around Olivia, hugging her tight against his body, aware of the raging emotions that had to be rushing inside her. She had more to lose than anyone else in the town at the moment. In the next few minutes she would either have her son back or she would be forever broken by the loss of her little boy.

He also couldn't help but worry about Olivia's personal safety. If things went bad, there was a possibility she might catch a bullet as well as any of them.

She shivered slightly against him and he tightened his arm around her shoulder. It had been incredibly brave of her to leave the safe house, to leave behind the one child she had in her possession and come here. It was the kind of bravery that assured him that somehow, someway, no matter how this night turned out, she would survive. He'd have to make certain of that fact.

He tensed as he heard the faint whisper of footsteps approaching. "Micah?" His name was a mere whisper, but he recognized Hawk's voice.

He peeked out from behind the tree. "We're here," he whispered in return and motioned them to come closer. Hawk was with Agent Randy Avery. They had all agreed that the fewer people involved in this particular part of the operation the better.

The underground corridor that Micah had found had been empty and silent and he hoped to keep it that way. In and out, no trouble, no noise and definitely no drama. Get the kids to safety and then let the entire town explode apart as the FBI moved in to take over.

By the end of this operation, Olivia should have her

son back, Samuel should be in custody and the town could begin the healing process it desperately needed. It would take months, potentially years, before the town returned to some semblance of normal.

"We'll wait for the bell to ring," Micah said in a soft whisper. "And then I'll go in. The tunnel is long and the place where I saw the room and heard Ethan cry is about halfway between here and Samuel's house. It will take us a few minutes to reach the room."

"Us?" In the tiny glow of a penlight, Hawk looked from Micah to Olivia.

"I'm going in with him," she said, her soft voice holding a steely strength that brooked no argument. "He'll need help with the children."

Hawk hesitated a moment and then nodded, apparently finding it wise not to argue with a desperate mother.

"I'll radio you if we find anything or anyone unexpected," Micah said. "Hopefully we execute fully with nobody being the wiser."

"Everyone else is in place," Randy said. "We have men ready to move in the minute Hawk or you gives them the command."

"Just make sure that Samuel doesn't somehow slip this noose," Micah replied, his blood hot as he even considered the possibility of Samuel evading their snare.

The church bell ringing halted all conversation. A surge of adrenaline filled Micah as he looked at Olivia. It was time to go in.

He motioned to Olivia that he'd go in first. With his gun in one hand, he used his other hand to move the bush aside, revealing the earthen stairs that led down. Drawing a deep breath, praying that this went as planned, Micah began down the stairs.

Olivia followed Micah down the stairs, the scent of the earth pressing in all around her. This wasn't the lit corridor that Micah had told her about. This was a mole's tunnel, small and dark with just Micah's pen-light to penetrate the darkness.

She imagined her heartbeat crashing in the silence, alerting anyone in the area that she was near. She drew deep breaths through her nose in an effort to calm her nerves, to slow the beating of her heart. She had to remain cool and collected. The last thing Ethan needed was a hysterical, out-of-control mommy riding to his rescue.

It seemed as if they walked forever amid the scent of dank earth when finally ahead Olivia saw a faint glow of light.

The corridor! Just like Micah had explained, and in that corridor was a room that he'd believed held the children. Ethan! Her heart cried out his name, her arms ached with her need to grab him to her, to feel him against her heart.

What if the children had been moved? What if they burst into the room and there was nobody there? No, she couldn't think that way. This had to be the place. She had to get her son back right now.

As they reached the wider corridor, Micah motioned ahead where she could see the door on their right. Despite her attempt to control her excitement, she couldn't halt a rush of adrenaline that filled her. She suddenly felt strong enough to break open a locked door, to face a giant and beat him down to get to Ethan.

Micah reached back and touched her arm, as if he felt the energy that rolled off her and needed to calm her. Step by step they approached the door.

There was no window, no way to tell who or what lay behind, but as they got close enough for Micah to touch the doorknob, Olivia heard the faint cry of a child.

The sound shot straight to her womb, the piercing ache of maternal need. She couldn't be sure that it was her son that she heard, but the mournful cry threatened to break her heart.

As Micah opened the door and entered the room in a crouched position, his gun held in both hands in front of him, Olivia moved right behind him, her brain working overtime to take in the scene before them.

The room was definitely a nursery, with a playpen, a crib and a small toddler bed along the walls. In the center of the room was a child-sized table with crayons and paper and a bowl of what appeared to be applesauce.

There was a dark-haired, dark-eyed little boy in the crib and next to him was a familiar woman who jumped to her feet at their entrance.

"Wilma," Olivia exclaimed in stunned surprise. She assumed the child in the crib was Devin Black, but there was no sight of any other child. Oh, God, where was Ethan?

"Are you alone?" Micah asked, his gun not wavering from the older woman.

She nodded, but her gaze slid to a second doorway in the room. Micah muttered a curse beneath his breath, advanced on the closed door and disappeared into the other room.

"Wilma, how could you?" Olivia asked the woman who had worked at the day care center, the woman she had trusted to take care of her children each day that Olivia went to work. "How could you be a part of this?"

Before Olivia could say another word, Wilma flew across the room, slammed her into the wall and wrapped her skinny fingers around Olivia's neck.

The shock of the old woman's action momentarily rendered Olivia helpless and, as the air was squeezed out of her lungs, her knees buckled beneath her.

Olivia couldn't make a noise as the surprisingly strong hands pressed tighter against her throat. "I'm getting paid a lot of money for my work," Wilma hissed as her fingernails bit into Olivia's flesh.

Black dots began to dance in front of Olivia's eyes and she realized if she didn't do something fast, she'd never get the chance to see Ethan again, to hold his little body close, to see his beautiful smile.

Tears blurred her vision as darkness began to creep in and suddenly Wilma was gone, plucked from her like a piece of unwanted lint by a silent, but raging Micah. He whirled the old woman away and she hit the wall and slumped down, obviously dazed.

In that instant a wave of despair swept over Olivia. Although she was happy that apparently they'd found Devin Black, where was her Ethan?

Suddenly his little blond head peeked around the corner of the room where Micah had gone. "Ethan!" Olivia gasped and crouched as he ran to her and slammed into her arms. She hugged him tight, weeping quietly with a combination of both joy and relief.

"Come on, we've got to get out of here," Micah said.

She nodded and stood and hurried to the crib where she lifted out Devin and then grabbed Ethan by the hand. "We have to be very quiet," she told the boys as Micah hurried them from the room in front of him.

Devin clung to her like a frightened little monkey as Ethan squeezed her fingers painfully tight. They raced toward the exit as fast as possible with the two kids in tow.

"Hey…hey, you! Stop or I'll shoot!" The deep voice came from just behind them.

They turned to see Chief of Police Bo Fargo racing toward them, his broad face bright red with rage. Olivia gasped as instead of running for the exit, Micah raced toward the chief of police.

"Micah!" she screamed just as Bo fired his gun. The shot went wild, missing Micah who kicked the gun out of Bo's hand. At the same time Bo threw himself on Micah and the two tumbled to the floor.

Olivia froze as she saw Micah's gun skitter out of his hand and along the corridor floor. Should she grab the gun? Run and get the children to safety? Love for Micah exploded inside her. She didn't just want her son back, she wanted Micah to be safe, as well.

At that moment Micah threw a flurry of punches that stunned Bo and left him inert on the floor. Micah grabbed Bo's handcuffs, rolled the big man on his stomach and cuffed his hands behind his back.

"Go," he said urgently to Olivia as he grabbed his gun and raced toward her. They left the corridor and raced toward the earthen womb that would eventually take them up to the surface, up to safety.

Devin cried softly, clinging to her in frantic desperation as Ethan scampered bravely next to her. She breathed a sigh of relief as they reached the stairs that led upward.

Hawk was there and immediately took Devin into his arms, while Olivia grabbed up Ethan and hugged him tight, tears streaming down her face.

"We heard a gunshot," Hawk said.

"Chief of Police Fargo is currently cuffed on the floor. He got off a shot that fortunately didn't connect," Micah said as he exited the hole in the ground. "Now, get them to the safe house. Keep them safe, Hawk."

Olivia looked at Micah in surprise. "Aren't you coming with us?"

"Not yet. I've got to be sure that Samuel doesn't get away," he said.

"Leave it for the other men," Olivia said, her fear for him all consuming.

"I can't. I've got to see this through." He looked at Hawk. "Take good care of them for me, Hawk. Hopefully I'll see you later."

Randy took Devin from Hawk and Hawk took Ethan from Olivia's arms. "Come on, we're going to be moving fast," Hawk said.

"Olivia." She turned to look at Micah, his face lit with Hawk's small penlight. His eyes shone with a softness she'd never seen before, a softness that was like a whisper inside her heart, a caress in her soul. "I'll never forget you," he said. And then he was gone.

Chapter 13

The minute Micah hit the town's main street, he knew the raid was in full progress. People ran wildly from the Community Center as men wearing jackets identifying them as FBI attempted to round up as many as possible.

Gunfire resounded in the air, along with frantic screams that created the kind of chaos everyone had hoped to avoid. Micah ran to one of the blue-jacketed agents who had a seemingly bewildered Mayor Rufus Kittridge under arrest. "Did they get Samuel?"

"Last I heard he went down his rabbit hole, but don't worry, we have a guy on the other end of the tunnel waiting for him to pop up."

Micah cursed, angry that Samuel had managed to slip through the initial raid and not trusting a single agent to be able to keep Samuel down in his hole.

With his adrenaline pumping, he took off running.

He'd fulfilled his promise to Olivia. She had Ethan back and Dr. Rafe Black and Darcy would get the happy ending they'd dreamed of if the other little boy proved to be Devin. And Micah couldn't imagine the child being anyone else.

Now it was time for Micah to take care of his final business and a reckless energy carried him along the mountain where he knew the tunnel from the Community Center came up behind a large rock structure.

He wanted to be there before Samuel came above ground and disappeared into the forest. He needed to be there to stop Samuel from somehow managing to escape.

As he ran, his mind tumbled with a million thoughts. Samuel had stolen the very soul of a town. He'd taken children from their parents, destroyed families and killed innocent people. If he wasn't caught he'd do it all again, in another state, in another small town and that couldn't be allowed to happen.

Personally, he'd stolen Micah's ability to love, his ability to feel love. When he'd taken Johanna away, he'd broken something vital in Micah.

Olivia. Her name sang through his soul even as he tripped over a hidden vine and nearly fell to the ground. Maybe in a different time, in a different place, he would have accepted what he felt in his heart for her—love.

But as he raced through the bramble bushes, tore through the brush and around trees, he carried with him the knowledge that he might not survive the night, that he had nothing to offer Olivia and her children. He knew that he loved her enough to let her go to find her future somewhere else, with somebody else.

The fact that he'd already let go of Olivia only shot his rage toward his brother even higher. Gasping and out of breath, he finally reached the rock structure behind which hid the tunnel egress from the Community Center.

His heart crashed to a halt as he saw the FBI agent dead on the ground near the exit. A knife protruded from his chest. Samuel had already come up. Micah knelt down beside the dead agent and felt his wrist. Still warm, and with the cold night air, that meant Samuel was surely only minutes ahead of Micah.

There was no way Samuel knew the forest like Micah did. Samuel was probably dressed in his fancy business suit and slick Italian loafers. Not exactly survivalist clothing.

Micah stopped and held his breath, straining his ears to hear any movement that might indicate his brother's presence. Straight ahead in the distance he heard the crash and crackle of something or somebody moving fast.

His heartbeat quickened as he hurried toward the noise. Samuel probably didn't know that he was running up the mountain toward the cliff that overlooked the town he had owned.

Micah prayed he didn't veer from his current direction. If he continued, he'd find himself stuck between a killer drop-off at a cliff and the brother he'd tried to have murdered. Dead end. Dead Samuel.

As Micah continued to track his brother's movements, he felt as if they were the only two people in the entire world. Cain and Abel. Micah didn't remember much about the biblical brothers, but he was pretty sure that Cain had nothing on Samuel when it came to wicked intent.

The clouds overhead parted and the shine of the moon filtered down, allowing Micah enough illumination to turn off his flashlight. He was in soldier mode now, calm and with his mind blank and his heartbeat slow and steady.

He didn't think about Samuel being his brother, rather the man he hunted. The man he chased was a faceless, nameless enemy. It was nothing personal, simply business that had to be taken care of and he couldn't allow the enemy to leave the mountain.

He had no idea if his enemy was armed. Micah had his gun, but despite everything that Samuel had done, Micah wasn't sure he could look his brother in his eyes and shoot him. That would be too easy.

Samuel would hate being locked up, put away in a prison where he had no power, where he had no flock to lead, no kingdom to rule. He would hate wearing a jumpsuit instead of his fancy silk shirts and sharing a communal shower with dozens of murderers and rapists.

Micah stopped once again, realizing he'd almost reached the cliff. He crouched and moved slowly, cautiously and in a shaft of moonlight he saw his brother there, at the edge of the cliff, looking down on the town he'd built, on the town he owned and the mayhem he'd thought he'd escaped.

As Micah stepped out of the woods and into the small clearing where Samuel stood, his brother whirled around to face him.

"Ah, and so it ends the way it began, with just the

two of us all alone," Samuel said with a charming smile. "Are you going to shoot me with that gun?"

"Only if you force me to," Micah replied. "The difference between you and me is that I'll do my own dirty work instead of sending a minion."

"I don't know what you're talking about," Samuel scoffed. "I don't have minions. I can't help it that people respect me and want to follow my teachings."

"It's just us now, Samuel. There's nobody else around so it's not necessary for you to put on your act."

Samuel's smile fell as he gazed at Micah in speculation. "How much money would it take for you to let me walk off this mountain?" he asked, his eyes narrowing as he stared down Micah.

A dry laugh escaped Micah. "You don't have that much money, but you can start by telling the truth. You killed those women, didn't you?"

"I don't know what you're talking about," Samuel said as he took a step backward, coming precariously close to the edge of the cliff.

"Cut the crap," Micah said impatiently. He needed closure. He needed to know what had happened to those women, what had happened to Johanna. It was the last piece of a puzzle that he wanted to know.

Samuel studied him as if he were a peculiar specimen beneath a microscope slide. "They were supposed to be my women. Their allegiance was supposed to be to me, but one by one they pulled away, they started to work against me." He said the words as if amazed that such a thing could happen. "Don't you understand? I had to get rid of them. They each threatened all that I had built here. They tried to undermine what I had worked so hard to control." He shrugged. "Sometimes sacrifices have to be made for the greater good."

"For *your* greater good," Micah replied, trying to control the rage of emotions that shook his insides.

"I'm not going to prison." Samuel took another step toward the cliff and it was at that moment, Micah knew his brother would rather jump to his own death than face a day in jail. And Micah was just as determined that Samuel wouldn't get his easy out.

He anticipated Samuel's move, dropped his gun and leaped forward on his stomach to the ground as Samuel stepped off the edge of the cliff. He managed to grab his brother's wrist as he hung over the abyss.

Micah's entire body began to tremble with the strain of hanging on and keeping Samuel alive and as he gazed into the cult leader's eyes, he saw the panic of a man who wanted to live, but was willing to die if he had to face the consequences of his crimes.

"Let me go," Samuel said.

"Not a chance," Micah said, sweat running into his eyes and down the sides of his face as he hunkered against the earth with Samuel's weight threatening to drag him forward. Micah wrapped a leg around a nearby young tree trunk and grabbed Samuel's wrist with both hands, determined not to let him fall.

"She was a virgin, you know," Samuel said, his voice a sly purr. "Johanna, she was a sweet virgin when I first took her and I used her every day until she was all worn out."

A red curtain of blind rage swept over Micah. There was nothing more he wanted to do than release his hold, allow Samuel to fall down the side of the mountain and die. Samuel laughed, as if he knew Micah's torment and reveled in it.

Drop him, a little voice whispered. Just let him go. It would be so easy. It would all be done. Samuel would be done.

With a roar and a burst of nearly inhuman strength, driven by a rage he'd never felt before, Micah pulled up Samuel over the lip of the cliff and then collapsed into a boneless heap.

"Good job," Hawk said as he stepped from the woods. He slammed his foot into Samuel's back and pulled out a pair of handcuffs.

Auras danced in front of Micah's eyes as he slowly sat up, watching dully as Hawk hauled Samuel to his feet and cuffed his hands behind him.

"He's responsible for all the murdered women," Micah said, fighting the building, nauseating pound in the side of his head. "He confessed to me."

"He's lying," Samuel replied indignantly. "I wouldn't confess to something I didn't do. He's crazy. He shoved me off the cliff and tried to kill me."

Randy and another FBI agent entered the clearing. Randy grabbed Samuel as Hawk gave him a smile of amusement. "It's a funny thing about working a case where you don't know exactly who you can trust. I learned early in my career that there was only one way to make sure there were never any misunderstandings."

He pulled a small tape recorder from his pocket. "It's running now as we speak and it was taping when you told your brother about having to get rid of those women." He turned to his men. "You know what to do, so take off."

Micah was vaguely aware of the two agents leaving with Samuel. Hawk crouched down next to Micah. "I thought you were going to let him go."

"I wanted to. God, I can't tell you how much I wanted to, but death is way too easy for him. It was what he wanted and this time he wasn't going to win." The speech left Micah depleted, sickened by his migraine, and as he lay back against the cool grass, he knew no more.

It was the middle of the night. Ethan was sleeping in the little bed next to his brother's crib after spending the last hour cradled in her arms.

"I tried really hard to be brave," he'd said to her earlier, before he'd dropped off to sleep. "I knew you wouldn't forget about me even though Mrs. Lathrop said I was going to go live with a new family."

"I would never, ever let that happen," Olivia had replied as she'd hugged him close. She'd sat with him until he'd fallen asleep and only then had she gone into the kitchen to see what the news was from town.

Unfortunately, there was no news. There was only June at the table. Darcy had gone into town to meet Rafe the minute Hawk had placed Devin into her arms.

Jesse was outside standing guard at the entrance to make sure that none of the Devotees escaping from town and up into the mountains found their way inside the safe house.

Now that Ethan was where he belonged, there was only one person that filled Olivia's head, that filled her heart. Micah. Where was he? Was he okay? A new ache of absence had taken up residence inside her.

I'll never forget you. That's what he'd said as she, Hawk and Randy had hurried away with the children. *I'll never forget you.* What exactly did that mean? Did it mean he loved her? Were those simple words supposed to last her a lifetime? It hadn't been enough.

With each hour of night that ticked by, her concern grew more intense. What was happening in the "perfect" town of Cold Plains? Had the FBI managed to arrest all of Samuel's minions? Was Samuel now in custody? Where was Micah? Why hadn't he returned to the safe house?

Breakfast came and went as did an uneasy lunch. Nobody had come in who had been in town the night before. Hawk hadn't checked in, Micah was still gone and Olivia felt as if she was slowly losing her mind.

After lunch, with both boys down for naps, Olivia was desperate to talk to somebody, to anybody who had been in town and could tell her what had happened. She needed to know what had happened to Micah.

"Once things settle down, they'll probably relocate you and the boys," June said. The two women were seated at the table and the cave rang with an unusual silence.

Olivia shook her head. "I'm not going anywhere until I get some answers."

"Jesse said he'd heard radio talk that the FBI have twenty people under arrest." She hesitated a minute and then continued, "But there's been no word about either Samuel or Micah. Nobody seems to know what happened to the two of them."

"So, they didn't arrest Samuel with the others?" Olivia's heart sank.

"Maybe by now they have," June replied hopefully. "Maybe that's what's taken Micah so long to get back here."

Olivia grasped onto the hope that at any minute Micah would walk through the door. Even though she had Ethan back, she couldn't move forward until she knew the fate of the man who had been responsible for his return. Even though she knew there was no future with Micah, she had to know what had happened to the man she loved.

Night had fallen and the boys were once again in bed when not Micah, but Hawk came into the safe house. He appeared weary beyond exhaustion as he sank down at the table with June, Jesse and Olivia.

"What's the news from town?" June asked anxiously.

"Is Samuel in jail?" Olivia asked.

Hawk shook his head, his jaw tense. "Samuel escaped into the mountains. We've arrested Wilma Lathrop and Bo Fargo, who have told us that they were behind the kidnapping and adoption scheme of the children. They insist that Samuel knew nothing about it."

"So, once again he's like the Teflon king and you all won't have any real charges to press against him when he eventually resurfaces," June said in disgust.

"We've cut off a lot of his tentacles. One of his main henchmen, Dax Roberts, the man who shot Micah months ago, is dead after a gun battle with an agent. Most of his other known men have been arrested. All the Devotees are going to be lost and questioning where to turn from here."

Olivia was glad Dax Roberts was dead. He'd tried

to kill Micah and now had paid the ultimate price for his allegiance with the devil.

Hawk leaned back in his chair and swept a hand through his sandy hair, his brown eyes holding a bone weariness. "We still don't know how deep the corruption ran. We can't know after this initial sweep if we got everyone who needed to be arrested. But it was a start, and if Samuel does return, he'll have his work cut out for him rebuilding what he once had."

Olivia felt as if she might explode. He was talking about people she didn't care about and hadn't once mentioned the name of the man she needed to know about most of all. She could stand it no longer.

"Micah." His name burst from her lips. "Where is Micah?"

Hawk's eyes darkened. "Actually, I came by here to see if I could borrow you for a while. There's someplace I need to take you."

Olivia stared at him, her heart in her throat. "Where? Where do you want to take me?"

He looked around at the others at the table. "Just come with me, Olivia. Don't ask questions. Trust me, this is something that has to be done."

Something that had to be done? Like saying goodbye to a dead man? Fear leaped into her throat, bitter and vile tasting.

"I'll keep an eye on the boys," June said gently. "There's no reason to pull them from their sleep."

Olivia stared at her blankly. Was Micah dead? Did Hawk want to take her to where his body was to give her final closure?

On wooden legs she rose as Hawk also stood. She

wanted to know now. She needed to know at this moment if Micah was dead or alive, but Hawk's eyes were dark and hooded, closed off to any more questions she might have.

June got up from the table and gave Olivia a hug. "Don't worry about the boys. They'll be fine here." As she released Olivia, her eyes held a sympathy Olivia didn't want to acknowledge.

She grabbed a jacket against the cold night air and followed Hawk as he left the safe house and down the mountain to a street on the outskirts of Cold Plains where a car awaited them.

Hawk got behind the wheel as she slid into the passenger seat, her heart thudding with a dread that made her feel nauseous. "Are you going to tell me where we're going?" she finally asked as he pulled away and headed out of town.

"Unfortunately I don't have the clearance to tell you anything. I'm just following orders."

Orders? Orders from whom? She loved Micah and if he was dead, he'd given his life all for nothing. Samuel was on the loose and there were still criminals walking the streets of Cold Plains.

Even though he'd told her he wasn't cut out to be a husband or father, there had been a part of her that had retained hope that somehow she could change his mind, that he would love her more than he feared a romantic commitment.

Now that hope was gone. But she reminded herself that his death hadn't all been in vain. Ethan was back where he belonged, as was Devin Black. If Micah was dead, then he'd died a hero.

This thought was little comfort as she fought against the tears that burned at her eyes. As she stared out into the darkness, she realized they were on the highway that would take them into the town of Laramie.

She frowned over at Hawk, who hadn't said a word for the last forty minutes. Was it possible that Micah wasn't dead but rather had been sent to the hospital here with grave wounds?

Was Hawk giving her a chance to tell Micah a final goodbye before he died? Her heart squeezed so tight at the thought she could barely draw her next breath.

When they reached the town, Hawk pulled up in front of a three-story hotel and stopped the engine. He turned to look at her, his eyes gleaming with a kindness that was nearly her undoing.

He pulled a room card key from his pocket and handed it to her. "Room 212. Everything will be explained. Now, go."

She got out of the car, unsure if she was walking into disaster or something else. Nerves jumped inside her stomach as she proceeded, unsteady on her feet, across the lobby floor and punched the elevator button for the second floor.

What was going on here? Why was she here? As the elevator doors whooshed opened, she stepped inside, heart pounding and nerves screaming just beneath the surface of her skin.

When she reached the second floor, she exited the elevator and walked down the hallway to 212. She paused outside the door, afraid to go inside, afraid not to. What or who was behind the door?

She slid the key through the slot and saw the green

light flicker to let her know she could open the door. With a deep breath, she pushed it open and realized the room was a compact suite. The space she entered was like a small living room and a man she'd never seen before jumped up from the sofa, a gun pointed at her.

She squeaked a surprise and he immediately lowered the gun. "Olivia Conner?" he asked.

She nodded and at that moment the door to the bedroom opened and Micah appeared. With a sharp gasp she ran toward him, slamming into his big, strong body as his arms wrapped tightly around her.

"I thought you were dead," she said and began to weep.

He pulled her into the bedroom and closed the door behind them with her still in the embrace of his arms.

"As far as you and the boys are concerned, I am dead. I just couldn't let you go without saying a final goodbye." His voice was a husky whisper in her hair.

She raised her head to look at him. "I don't want to say goodbye. I love you, Micah. I love you with all my heart and soul." The words spilled from her, unable to stay inside her another minute. "I know you love me, too. I see it when you look at me, I feel it with every part of me. Let it be, Micah, don't fight against it."

She saw his love now, shining from his eyes. "Go with us. Relocate with us and build a life," she continued. "Be the husband, the father that you were meant to be. You deserve to be loved, Micah, and you deserve happiness. We can give that to you. Let yourself accept it."

He disentangled from her and took a step backward, his eyes pools of tortured emotions. "There's more at play here than just you and me." He walked over to the edge of the bed and sat down, then patted the space next to him.

Olivia sank down, her head filled with the clean male scent of him, her heart aching with the wealth of love for him that felt too big for her chest.

"There's much to be done in Cold Plains," he said, as if that somehow explained everything. "We know we didn't get everyone who has dirty hands."

"What are you saying? That you're going to stay here and continue to work with the FBI?"

He hesitated a moment and then slowly nodded. "That's the plan."

"But you know Samuel will come back and if he knows you're here, he'll try to have you killed again," she protested.

Micah was silent for a long moment, his gaze holding hers intently. "What I'm about to tell you is top secret information. You can't share it with anyone. Soon enough June and Jesse will know along with a few key players in town, but that's it."

"Okay," she said slowly, her heart once again beating an unsteady rhythm.

"The official story is that Samuel escaped the FBI net and with Bo and Wilma proclaiming his innocence in the adoption scheme, there's nothing to arrest him for. As for me, I died on the mountain, shot by persons unknown."

"And the unofficial story?" she asked softly.

"Samuel is in custody," he replied. She listened as he told her of the battle that had taken place on the cliff, a chill shivering through her as she realized how close

Micah had come to death. While he'd been trying to keep Samuel alive, he could have been pulled over the cliff's edge and both brothers would have been killed.

"He confessed to me to being responsible for the death of all those women." He explained to her about the final moments of Samuel's freedom, how he'd proclaimed his innocence and Hawk's tape recorder that had caught the confession on tape.

"By the time Samuel was led away by a couple agents, I had passed out from a migraine." He frowned, as if hating the weakness that had been left behind when his brother had tried to have him killed.

"When I finally came to, Hawk was seated next to me. He told me that Samuel had been taken to a secret location and I was to come with him. And here I am."

"So, Samuel is gone. Why would you have to stick around here? You accomplished what you wanted," she said, trying to understand why he was here in this hotel, why the official word was that he was dead. And then she knew.

"I love you, Olivia. I want the best for you and your sons. I have another mission to accomplish and I battle migraines. I'm no good for you. I love you enough to let you go, even though it's killing me right now." His voice trembled with emotion and it was in the depth of emotion that she saw her future.

"I get cramps," she said. "Every once in a while I get stomach cramps and all I want to do is stay in bed with a heating pad. I have a mission to accomplish, too. I want my boys to know the love and guidance of a good man. I want a man who makes me feel strong and vibrant and passionate and that man is you. If you are planning on staying in Cold Plains, then so am I. I have a nice house waiting for my return. The Community Center will still need a secretary and you can't beat the scenery in town."

"Olivia…"

She placed a finger against his lips. "I know exactly what I'm getting into, Micah, and I'm all in. Don't throw us away. We need you, and I have a feeling you need us, too."

His eyes shimmered with a light that nearly stole her breath away. "I do need you, Olivia. I feel as if I've waited my entire life for you and those little boys to come along. I don't know much about being a husband and nothing about being a parent, but I do know that I love you and I'll do everything in my power to keep you and the boys safe and happy."

Tears of joy shimmered in her eyes. "That's all I need, Micah. We'll figure it out as we go. I think our two missions might work together very well."

He stood and pulled her off the bed and into his embrace. "I learned early in my life not to give my heart to anyone, but somehow you managed to get in under my defenses. You have my heart, Olivia."

She leaned into him and smiled. "And I'll take very good care of it."

He took her mouth with his in a searing kiss that spoke not only of tenderness and passion, of commitment and caring, but also of a future together that would contain all the things that made up dreams.

Olivia knew the next weeks and months might be difficult, but at the end of each day she'd find her comfort in Micah's arms and her sons would find the father they needed.

It didn't matter if Cold Plains was a "perfect" town or not. She'd found the perfect man to be her life partner and together they would build a life on the foundation of love.

Epilogue

It had been a week since the raid on the small town of Cold Plains, and in that week much had happened to forever change Darcy Craven's life.

Deputy Ford McCall had finally identified Jane Doe as not only being Catherine George, but also the woman who had given birth to Darcy.

Darcy now walked with Rafe through the cemetery where her mother had been buried the day before. Rafe pushed the stroller with Devin gurgling the nonsensical, but pleasant sounds of babyhood.

Darcy carried in her arms a bouquet of daisies. Daisies were Darcy's favorite flowers and somehow she believed her mother had loved them, too.

Although she was heartbroken that she'd never have the reunion she'd dreamed about with her mother, she was comforted by the fact that her mother had taken her to Louise to protect her, to save her from the evil man who was her father.

It had taken tremendous love and sacrifice for Catherine to leave Darcy behind and in many ways Darcy would be forever grateful to the mother she'd never had the opportunity to get to know.

As they drew closer to the grave site, Rafe stopped at a stone bench nearby. "Go ahead," he said to her. "Take a little time by yourself."

She nodded, grateful that he understood her need to just stand, to just be in the spiritual presence of her mother. She walked a few more steps and stopped in front of the headstone that read *Catherine George* with the years of her birth and death. Below that were the words *Beloved Mother*.

"Beloved mother," Darcy whispered softly as she leaned down and gently placed the flowers on the grave. "Thank you for being strong enough, for being brave enough, to save me." She straightened up, a piercing sadness in her heart, but also a sense of pride. There was no doubt in her mind that, along with her blue eyes, she'd gotten her inner strength from her mother.

She stood there for several minutes, allowing the pain of loss to peak and then slowly recede away. It was time to put the past behind her. She and Rafe had made the decision to stay on in Cold Plains. Rafe wanted to continue his medical practice and she would continue as his receptionist and watch Devin, who had gained her heart the moment he was placed in her arms. Rafe was a good man and Cold Plains was a town that desperately needed good men.

She turned now and gazed at the two men who held not only her heart, but also her future. Rafe smiled and suddenly she wanted away from this place. Yes, it was time to put the past behind her and focus on the future, her wonderful future with Rafe and Devin.

"All done," the man said as he took the cape off Micah's shoulders and brushed him down with a soft-bristled brush. When he was finished, Micah stood and straightened the collar of the white dress shirt he wore. The shirt cost more than any item of clothing Micah had ever owned, as did the suit coat he shrugged on. It was like donning another man's skin.

As the barber left him alone in the room, Micah closed his eyes and thought of Olivia and her boys. They had settled back in the house where she'd lived before her world had exploded apart and Micah couldn't wait for the time they could be together again and that was going to be soon…very soon.

He'd been told that while things were relatively calm in Cold Plains, everyone appeared to be uneasy, waiting to see what happened next. They were a flock without a shepherd, a group of bewildered people seeking leadership.

Micah knew what happened next.

He slowly turned around and gazed at his reflection in the dresser mirror. The barber had done a perfect job styling his new short haircut. The suit fit him as if tailored specifically for him.

The resemblance was now uncanny. The flock needed a shepherd and he was about to return.

Micah smiled at his reflection, aware that his new mission was about to begin. "Hello, Samuel," he said softly.

* * * * *

HRSCNM0612

REQUEST YOUR FREE BOOKS!
2 FREE NOVELS PLUS 2 FREE GIFTS!

ROMANTIC
SUSPENSE

Sparked by Danger, Fueled by Passion.

YES! Please send me 2 FREE Harlequin® Romantic Suspense novels and my 2 FREE gifts (gifts are worth about $10). After receiving them, if I don't wish to receive any more books, I can return the shipping statement marked "cancel." If I don't cancel, I will receive 4 brand-new novels every month and be billed just $4.49 per book in the U.S. or $5.24 per book in Canada. That's a saving of at least 14% off the cover price! It's quite a bargain! Shipping and handling is just 50¢ per book in the U.S. and 75¢ per book in Canada.* I understand that accepting the 2 free books and gifts places me under no obligation to buy anything. I can always return a shipment and cancel at any time. Even if I never buy another book, the two free books and gifts are mine to keep forever.

240/340 HDN FEFR

Name	(PLEASE PRINT)	
Address		Apt. #
City	State/Prov.	Zip/Postal Code

Signature (if under 18, a parent or guardian must sign)

Mail to the **Reader Service:**
IN U.S.A.: P.O. Box 1867, Buffalo, NY 14240-1867
IN CANADA: P.O. Box 609, Fort Erie, Ontario L2A 5X3

Not valid for current subscribers to Harlequin Romantic Suspense books.

Want to try two free books from another line?
Call 1-800-873-8635 or visit www.ReaderService.com.

* Terms and prices subject to change without notice. Prices do not include applicable taxes. Sales tax applicable in N.Y. Canadian residents will be charged applicable taxes. Offer not valid in Quebec. This offer is limited to one order per household. All orders subject to credit approval. Credit or debit balances in a customer's account(s) may be offset by any other outstanding balance owed by or to the customer. Please allow 4 to 6 weeks for delivery. Offer available while quantities last.

Your Privacy—The Reader Service is committed to protecting your privacy. Our Privacy Policy is available online at www.ReaderService.com or upon request from the Reader Service.

We make a portion of our mailing list available to reputable third parties that offer products we believe may interest you. If you prefer that we not exchange your name with third parties, or if you wish to clarify or modify your communication preferences, please visit us at www.ReaderService.com/consumerschoice or write to us at Reader Service Preference Service, P.O. Box 9062, Buffalo, NY 14269. Include your complete name and address.

*Harlequin Intrigue® presents a new installment
in* USA TODAY *bestselling author
Delores Fossen's miniseries*
THE LAWMEN OF SILVER CREEK RANCH.

Enjoy a sneak peek at KADE.

Kade saw it then. The clear bassinet on rollers, the kind
they used in the hospital nursery.

He walked closer and looked inside. There was a baby,
and it was likely a girl, since there was a pink blanket snuggled around her. There was also a little pink stretchy cap on
her head. She was asleep, but her mouth was puckered as if
sucking a bottle.

"What does the baby have to do with this?" Kade asked.

"Everything. Two days ago someone abandoned her in the
E.R. waiting room," the doctor explained. "The person left
her in an infant carrier next to one of the chairs. We don't
know who did that, because we don't have security cameras."

Kade was finally able to release the breath he'd been
holding. So this was job related. They'd called him in because he was an FBI agent.

But he immediately rethought that.

"An abandoned baby isn't a federal case," Kade clarified,
though Grayson already knew that. Kade reached down and
brushed his index finger over a tiny dark curl that peeked
out from beneath the cap. "You think she was kidnapped or
something?"

When neither the doctor nor Grayson answered, Kade
looked back at them. The anger began to boil through him.
"Did someone hurt her?"

"No," the doctor quickly answered. "There wasn't a
scratch on her. She's perfectly healthy as far as I can tell."

The anger went as quickly as it had come. Kade had handled the worst of cases, but the one thing he couldn't stomach was anyone harming a child.

"I called Grayson as soon as she was found," the doctor went on. "There were no Amber Alerts, no reports of missing newborns. There wasn't a note in her carrier, only a bottle that had no prints, no fibers or anything else to distinguish it."

Kade lifted his hands palms up. "That's a lot of no's. What do you know about her?" Because he was sure this was leading somewhere.

Dr. Mickelson glanced at the baby. "We know she's about three or four days old, which means she was abandoned either the day she was born or shortly after. She's slightly underweight, barely five pounds, but there was no hospital bracelet. We had no other way to identify her, so we ran a DNA test." His explanation stopped cold, and his attention came back to Kade.

So did Grayson's. "Kade, she's yours."

How does Kade react when he finds out the baby is his?

Find out in KADE.
Available this July wherever books are sold.

This summer, celebrate everything Western
with Harlequin® Books!

www.Harlequin.com/Western

INTRIGUE®

CELEBRATE

DEBRA WEBB'S

50TH COLBY TITLE WITH A SPECIAL BONUS SHORT STORY!

Colby Roundup, the story of one woman's determination to remember her past before time runs out, marks Debra Webb's 50th Colby title, and to celebrate Harlequin Intrigue® is giving you a special BONUS Colby companion short story included with this book!

The excitement begins July 2 wherever books are sold!

SPECIAL EDITION

Life, Love and Family

USA TODAY bestselling author

Leanne Banks

begins a heartwarming new miniseries

Royal Babies

When princess Pippa Devereaux learns that the mother of Texas tycoon and longtime business rival Nic Lafitte is terminally ill she secretly goes against her family's wishes and helps Nic fulfill his mother's dying wish. Nic is awed by Pippa's kindness and quickly finds himself falling for her. But can their love break their long-standing family feud?

THE PRINCESS AND THE OUTLAW

Available July 2012!
Wherever books are sold.

HSE65680